diary of a 6th grade ninja 9

the scavengers strike back

BY MARCUS EMERSON
AND NOAH CHILD

ILLUSTRATED BY DAVID LEE

EMERSON PUBLISHING HOUSE

This one's for Finn...

In outer space, no one can hear a ninja… but I guess if that ninja were any good, no one should hear him on Earth either.

The alarm to the space station was blaring so loudly that I could hardly think. The second that Naoki and I appeared in the corridor, the station's security system was triggered, launching an attack of brightly colored laser blasts.

With no time to find cover, I had to trust my instincts to avoid getting hit. Shutting my eyes, I used my keen ninja senses to dodge the lasers, and while it worked for a few seconds, I knew I couldn't keep it up long. I had to shut off the security system if Naoki and I were gonna make it out alive.

"Master!" Naoki's tiny voice said, cutting through the noise of small explosions around us. "The off switch! It's there! Beneath your feet!"

I looked down, surprised to see that my sidekick was right. What kind of security system had an off switch sitting out in the open? No wonder that place had problems.

I thrust my foot down, stomping on the switch.

It beeped twice, and then a computer's voice came from a hidden speaker. "Thank you for using 'Lancelot's Laser Blast Security System. If ya can't beat 'em, then blast 'em.'"

"That was easy…" I said. "*Too* easy."

1

"Do you have a plan, master?" Naoki asked, his voice barely a whisper. "Or... a *master* plan?" He giggled at his own joke.

Naoki was my newest sidekick.

After my old sidekick (Bennie, the t-rex) quit to play ukulele in a street band on Oahu, Naoki was quick to apply for the job.

Naoki's resume was just a bunch of pictures of garbage cans that he had kicked and punched. If he were anyone else, I would've tossed out his resume, but Naoki... was a *raccoon*. A *ninja* raccoon! His ninja mask was *grown* right on his *face! How sweet was that?*

"Yes, Naoki," I said, floating in place. "I've got a plan."

Naoki reached out his tiny raccoon hands, and pushed himself off the wall. "Would you mind telling me the plan? Or is it some kind of super secret thing that I'm just going to have to be patient about?"

Naoki was an amazing sidekick, but sometimes that rodent could be pushy.

I tried acting cool, but the truth was that I might've been a little annoyed because even though I had a plan, it wasn't *much* of a plan. "I figured we'd get into the space station, check out what's up with the power being out, and then deal with any intruders. Sound good to you?" I asked.

"Yes," Naoki answered, but I could tell that it *didn't* sound good to him.

My name is Chase Cooper, and I'm a sixth grade ninja... on a mission in deep space with a raccoon as my noob sidekick.

Naoki and I had been sent by the planet Earth to scope out EV07. It was a space station that humans put on the edge of the Milky Way galaxy, in hopes of making contact with alien life. It bums me out to say that the space station hadn't made contact with little green beings yet.

About a week before Naoki and I were floating in the empty corridor of EV07, all communication to and from the station had been mysteriously cut off. Up until that moment, everything had been running smoothly.

The hope was that the station had just lost its primary communication systems and needed an upgrade, but in the real world, things were never that easy.

My raccoon sidekick and I had just arrived, not even ten

minutes earlier, by way of ninja teleportation. I'd totally tell you how to do it if I could, but you know… ninja secrets and stuff.

Ninja teleportation ain't even that big of a deal. Naoki and I first had to travel to one of Saturn's moons before we could teleport the rest of the way to the edge of the galaxy.

Now, I know what you're thinking – but Chase, if you can teleport hundreds of light-years across the galaxy, what was the point of going to Saturn? Like, was the distance just a *smidge* too far to handle simply teleporting straight from Earth?

My answer to that question? Yes. Yes, it was.

When we arrived, the power was completely out, like someone had left and shut off all the lights. But the thing about EV07 was that there weren't any humans aboard. It was the first space station entirely run by androids.

And because the power was out, the artificial gravity wasn't working. When Naoki and I got there, we found ourselves floating helplessly through one of the dark corridors in the west wing.

Boxes filled with random spaceship parts floated weightlessly around us as well. If we were on Earth, those boxes would have easily weighed a thousand pounds each, but since we were in space, they weighed nothing. I'd just have to remember to stay away from them when the artificial gravity was switched back on.

"First, we'll have to flip the switch to get some juice running through this ship's veins again," I said. "After that, we'll check out why the communication was cut off."

"Perhaps the communication was cut because the power went out?" Naoki suggested.

"I dunno," I said. "Maybe."

"You don't sound too convinced, master," Naoki said.

"There's just something odd about the whole thing," I said, running my fingers along the wall as I floated toward the end of the corridor. "This place is run by robots—"

Naoki cut me off. "*Androids*, master. You know they hate being called *robots*."

"Yes, of course," I groaned. "I'm sorry. *Androids…* were supposed to be running this place. Their power source isn't the same as EV07's, so when the *ship* shut down, the androids should've kept going. I mean, *they* should be the ones

around this boat trying to get her up and runnin' again, but...
have you seen any androids since we got here?"

Naoki didn't answer, but I heard the rustle of his fur,
which meant he was giving me an answer by shaking his head.
Then the raccoon spoke. "Welp," he said. "Now I'm kinda
freaked out."

"Naaah," I said, trying to sound like I wasn't bothered
by it. "We're just at the edge of the galaxy, hundreds of light
years away from a single other human being, floating down a
dark hallway on an abandoned space station. It's nothing!"

"Except that sounded like you were describing the plot
to a horror movie," Naoki whispered, his voice slightly
trembling. "The kind of horror movie where an abandoned
space station just came back from a place of pure evil... along
with a stowaway."

Just then, a low groaning sound came from the walls of
the space station. It was the same sound a house makes in the
middle of the night, when everything is dead silent, except for
a random *CREAAAAAAK* that comes from somewhere you
can't see, and then you look at your dad for comfort, but he's
just as wide-eyed as you are, staring at nothing and waiting to
see if the sound would repeat itself, and then you suddenly
realize you have to go to the bathroom, but there's no way
you're about to go all alone, and your dad shrugs his shoulders
and says something like, "Eh, it's just the house settling..."

Yeah, right, dad! I know what it sounds like when the
house is settling! And a weird groaning sound *isn't* that!

Um, I'm sorry. Anyways...

"That sounded spooky," I said.

"Really? Are you sure?" Naoki commented
sarcastically.

The groan came again, but this time from the end of the
dark hallway.

Floating helplessly, I snapped my attention at the
shadows only to see shadows *moving* in the shadows.

"Master!" Naoki cried. "Shadow ninjas! Throw me!"

"On it!" I said, grabbing one of my raccoon sidekick's
tiny paws.

Without any gravity, Naoki felt as light as a feather
when I brought his body over my head, shooting him down the
hallway.

Naoki rolled himself into a tight ball, keeping his knees

under his stomach. It was hard to see the shadow ninjas jumping back and forth through the corridor, but not impossible.

Zipping down the hall, Naoki shot through the shadow ninjas like a furry football, throwing his fists and feet out at the last second. But the attack didn't faze any of the ninjas. Naoki's raccoon body simply slipped through their black silhouettes like they were shadows because, well, that's *exactly* what they were.

My ninja buddy slammed into the glass door at the end of the corridor on the other side of the shadow ninjas and shouted a bunch of stuff in his native tongue that would probably be considered inappropriate if there were a translator nearby.

"Chase!" Naoki said as he peered through the frosted glass door. "I mean, *master!* Quickly! The bridge of the space station is in this next room!"

Drifting like lint caught in a small breeze, I continued moving toward the end of the dark corridor, toward the shadow ninjas.

"I see a light!" Naoki said. "There's a computer panel at the front of the bridge that has a blinking red dot! That *has* to be important, right? Like, the whole station should start back up because of that?"

"It sounds like something that's possible," I said, watching the shadow ninjas bounce off the walls. In the darkness, I couldn't tell how many there were, but I was pretty sure it was more than Naoki and I could handle.

"Wait," Naoki said. "It just occurred to me that it might just be the blinking red light to a smoke detector."

"It doesn't matter!" I said. "All that matters is that we get into that room!"

I spun in a circle, floating at the center of the corridor, and then ninja kicked the wall closest to me to get myself moving. With as strong as my flash kick was, I wasn't surprised that I was suddenly flying through the hall with immense speed.

The shadow ninjas slowed, crawling across the surface of the space station walls. Because the lights were out, it was like watching black objects move around on a black surface.

All at once, several of the shadow ninjas formed together, rising off the floor at the center of the room, creating the shape of a person that was much larger than a sixth grader.

"Master!" Naoki's strained voice said. "I've got the door open! Quickly! We must make haste!"

"Workin' on it!" I replied just as I got to the shadowy figure standing in my way.

I shielded my face, expecting to sift through the figure the same way Naoki had passed through the ninjas when they were still shadows, but I guess it didn't work like that.

The shadow ninja grabbed my wrist and spun in a circle, launching me toward one of the space station walls. Pain surged through my body as I bounced off the hard plastic.

Again, I found myself floating as I watched the figure fly toward me. Apparently the shadow ninja was able to move around in a weightless environment. He raised his fist, somehow making it grow to twice the size of a normal fist.

I was just far enough away from the walls that I couldn't reach them to try and move my body. Kicking my feet, I looked like a dog treading water, but without the water.

"Naoki!" I screamed, bicycle-kicking my legs.

If you've read anything about being in a gravity free place, then you'd know that it's nearly impossible to make yourself move in any direction unless you were able to push yourself off an object that was stuck in place. I could doggy paddle until I puked, but I wasn't going anywhere.

All I could do was watch the shadow ninja as he delivered his finishing move.

At that moment, there was a flash of light behind the shadow ninja, back at the bridge of the space station.

That same instant, the lights above flickered to life. My body fell hard to the floor.

The boxes that had been floating around Naoki and me when we first arrived crashed to the floor of the corridor, shaking the walls like there was an earthquake.

I jumped to my feet, ready to defend myself against the shadow ninja, but to my surprise, he wasn't there anymore. At least he wasn't *standing* anymore.

Under one of the giant boxes was the arm of my attacker, slowly vanishing into thin air, the same way steam does from a boiling pot of water.

"You dead?" Naoki's raccoon voice came from the down the hall.

"Just about," I replied. "I take it you found the lights then?"

Naoki chuckled. "Yeah! Turns out the blinking red light *was* the right button."

"Nice," I said, dusting myself off as I stood, even though there wasn't any dust on me. It was mostly just a reflex.

I joined Naoki on the bridge of the space station and studied our surroundings. Except for a few notches on the floor, everything seemed to be in tiptop shape.

The bridge to EV07 was a giant circle that was completely empty. Along the outside of the bridge were blinking computer panels and screens for crewmembers to work on.

At the very center of the floor was a blue glowing circle, pulsing slowly like it was breathing. The blue circle was the heart of the bridge, and created the holograms that made up the rest of the ship's control panels in the big empty space on the bridge.

The holograms controlled the rest of the systems that kept EV07 running smoothly, which was super cool to look at, because even though they were holograms, they felt like solid control panels. You could bump your knee on one if you weren't careful.

I walked out to the center of the bridge, tapping my foot

on the blue circle. "How do we get this thing to work, because I'd love to—"

A powerful light switched on from the back of the bridge, shining so bright that it was impossible to see anything. Even though the light was blinding, the room was silent. Like, crazy silent. *You-could-hear-a-pin-drop* kind of silent.

"Naoki?" I said, squeezing my eyes shut. "Can you see anything?"

I moved forward, but my thigh bumped into an object that had appeared out of nowhere. The holograms on the bridge had switched on!

"Master!" Naoki's voice said. "I'm stuck! Something's... got me!"

"Keep talking," I said. "I'll follow your voice."

"And if I speak over your friend?" another voice said from somewhere near the back of the room.

"Uh, Naoki?" I asked.

"Still here," Naoki said. "And that wasn't me."

The voice of the stranger belted out a laugh. "No, but it was me!"

"Who are you?" I asked, trying to move forward, but it was impossible. My legs were stuck on something solid, but I couldn't feel anything wrapped around my body. I looked behind me, at my shadow that was cast against the floor of the bridge. Holding onto the shadow of my ankles, were the shadow ninjas. They were keeping me in place by holding my own shadow hostage.

Naoki was being held prisoner by the shadow ninjas across the room as well.

Footsteps patted the ground as the stranger paced slowly back and forth. "Someone you know very well... and someone you hardly know at all."

"Yeah, okay," I said. "*That* makes sense."

The stranger stepped closer, but stayed hidden just outside the beam of light that was coming from the back of the bridge. He was only near enough that I could make out his shape. He was roughly the same size as me, which meant he was also a sixth grader, and over his face... was a black ninja mask.

"You know," the ninja said. "It's almost disappointing how easy it was to lure you out here to the edge of the galaxy. I honestly thought I'd have to go through with an incredibly elaborate plan to get you hundreds of light-years away from the Earth. I mean, I spent *weeks* on a plan! After this space station's power went out, I was gonna go ahead and start flipping the power on and off, hoping to catch someone's attention. After that, I was gonna reprogram all these robots to send video waves back to Earth, and… yadda, yadda, yadda! I won't bore you with the details!"

"So you've got me here," I said, annoyed. "What do you want?"

The bright spotlight dimmed most of the way, but didn't fully shut off. The shadow ninjas holding my ankles needed that light to cast my shadow, otherwise I'd break free from them.

The mystery ninja stepped around me at a distance that was just out of my reach. I studied the bridge of the ship, and the spotlight near the back. All along one of the computer terminals were several porcelain cups that looked way too fancy for a bunch of androids.

SPACE NINJA!
(STANDING ON THE BRIDGE OF A PRETTY SWEET SPACE STATION)

The ninja was wearing something over his face. It was probably a device to help him breath oxygen in deep space, but I don't think it was necessary since EV07 had air. Maybe he used it to walk outside the ship.

"Nice tea set," I said. "It's a surprising amount of pottery for a villain."

"What?" the ninja asked. His eyes told me there was a smile behind his mask. "Villains can't have nice things?"

The voice of the ninja was familiar to me. Like, I *knew* that I'd heard the kid talk before, but I just couldn't place who it was in my mind. It was familiar enough that I knew I was gonna feel stupid if I ever found out. It was a boy's voice, which meant that it wasn't the vampire queen Naomi, but it wasn't Wyatt either. I went through the list of kids who hated me – Jake? Nope. Sebastian? Nope. Carlyle? Nope. Mr. A. Lien? Because he caught me making fun of his name one time… but also nope.

"I can see the confusion in your eyes," the ninja said, stepping closer to me.

I blinked. "Maybe because that's all you can see of my face? Duh-doy."

Again, the ninja's eyes told me he was smiling. "You know me, Chase Cooper, but you can't quite put your finger on who I am yet, can you? It's right there, isn't it? On the *tip* of your tongue, but you just can't *even!*"

I said nothing, hating the fact that this ninja was able to tell what I was thinking. I was being too confident. I needed to harden up and hide all emotion from my eyes and my body language.

"I'll be honest with you," the ninja said. "You've looked me in the eye every single day, but you've never been able to see my *actual* eyes until now, in this space station."

"Okaaaaay?" I said, pretty confused.

"I've lived in darkness too long," the mystery ninja said, stepping even closer. His voice was maddeningly familiar. He reached out and pulled the mask off of my face. "But I'm ready to step into the light…and go home to Earth."

"Who are you?" I asked, feeling the cold air of EV07 on the bare skin of my face.

"Out of all the enemies you've ever had," the ninja went on. "I'm by far your worst. Surprisingly, I've been your worst enemy since you first became a ninja all those thousands of years ago in the woods behind Buchanan School…"

"Uh, no?" I said, trying to shake my ankles free from the shadow ninjas at my feet. "Pretty sure Wyatt was the bad guy back then. If I had some sort of unofficial foe, then I'd probably know about it, right?"

"Wrong," the ninja said coldly.

"And y'know what else? Even if you *do* make it back to Earth," I said. "They'll lock you up the instant you get there! All I have to do is send one video wave back to my bosses, and they'll put an alert out for you!"

"But Chase," the ninja said, stepping so close that his face was only a foot away from mine. "How are they gonna lock *me* up… when *I'm* the one who sent the video wave in the first place?"

The ninja grabbed the top of his mask. With a snap of his wrist, he yanked his ninja mask off his face.

The boy under the mask… the one whose voice was so familiar…

…was *me*.

ME VS. (EVIL) ME
BUT I HAVE TO ADMIT
HIS GOATEE IS
KINDA COOL!

I was staring, dumbfounded, at my own face as he smiled an evil smile back at me. Oh, and he also had a goatee, which I had to admit, looked pretty dashing.

"Mind. Blown," Naoki stated from across the room. "Chase, he must be a clone of you! Your *evil* clone!"

"But that's impossible!" I said. "All the way out here at the edge of the galaxy? If he were a clone of me, where'd he even get the *hair?*"

Naoki stopped, looking at me, puzzled. The ninja with my face did the same thing.

"You mean, like, the hair they used to clone you?" Naoki asked.

"No," I said. "The hair that's sitting on top of that kid's head right now."

The ninja with my face ran his fingers through his thick, black head of hair. "*This* hair?"

"Yeah!" I said. "If you're my clone, then where'd you even get that?"

Naoki and my evil clone looked at each other, super confused. Naoki shrugged his shoulders.

"That makes no sense," Naoki said quietly. "Like, *at all.*"

"You don't really understand how cloning works, do you?" the ninja asked.

I pouted, but, like, a *heroic* pout. "Yuh-huh."

My evil clone walked around me slowly. "You're broken, Chase. You've been cracked over and over, and now you're barely able to keep yourself together anymore."

"So that's it?" I asked. "You brought me here to break me?"

The clone nodded. "I'm the perfect version of you! Awesome and flawless. I'm going to replace you on Earth, but before anyone realizes I'm *not* you, the world will already be mine. Humanity will bow before my ninja fist!"

"Pretty sure my friends will know something's up because of that goatee," I huffed.

My clone stopped and narrowed his eyes at me. "I can always shave it off," he said as if that answer should've been obvious.

I bit my cheek out of frustration because he was right. "Dangit!" I grunted. "You know you're in a boatload of trouble when I get free from these shadow ninjas, right?"

12

"Then I suppose it's time for me to relieve you from your duty..." the clone said, "... of *living*."

"He said *doodie!*" Naoki laughed.

"Not helping, dude," I replied. I was beginning to wonder whether a raccoon was a poor choice of sidekick.

In a flash of black ninja clothing, my evil clone spun in a circle away from me, and floated in the air for a full second, charging himself up. And then he tightened his fists, and threw out his finishing move.

I tried to break free from the shadow ninjas grasping at my ankles, but it was no use. Raising my hands, I did my best to block the attack, but I was too late. My evil clone landed his punch square on my cheek...

But to my surprise, it barely hurt. Actually, it was more annoying than painful. It was kind of like a biscuit had hit me in the face.

And then I realized it *was* a biscuit that hit me.

I wasn't on some abandoned space station near the edge of the galaxy, but I *wished* I was. Instead of somewhere cool like that, I was in the lunchroom of Buchanan School, staring at a crumbly biscuit that was on the table in front of me.

Someone from the table next to mine had thrown it. I could tell because everyone over there was snickering and pointing fingers in my direction.

And then another biscuit came from the table, sailing high in the air until landing right on top of my head.

Great. What a way to start the week.

Monday. 7:25 AM. The cafeteria.

With some extra time to burn before school started, I thought it would be nice to grab some breakfast from the school's kitchen. Most of the time, breakfast alone in the cafeteria was a pretty quiet time, but for some reason that morning, a couple kids thought it'd be funny to chuck some biscuits at my face.

I think they still had a chip on their shoulder from the newsletter that was put out under my name a few weeks back - the one The Scavengers published that contained the secrets of every sixth grader in the school.

I'm pretty sure I'll still have enemies from that for a long time, maybe even when I graduated from high school.

Since I didn't feel like being a biscuit target for the kids at the next table, I scooped up my tray and headed for the trashcan at the side of the cafeteria.

I caught a glimpse of Naomi at the other end of the lunchroom. She was sitting alone, but she didn't notice me. Good thing too, because I probably would've looked away as soon as she did, which was the obvious clue that someone was staring at you.

    For the past couple weeks, it was like some secret part of my brain would find Naomi before I realized it. Whenever she was around, I knew exactly where she was before even looking at her. Sometimes I imagined a giant carnival sign with her name on it, hovering over her head, trying to get my attention.

    Naomi was taking a bite from a sausage biscuit. A juice box was sitting on the table in front of her, next to a small cup that looked like something from a child's tea party set. I wasn't sure what the cup was all about.

    Most of you know this already, but Naomi used to be one of my best friends. She was a strong member of my ninja clan who I had fun talking to even when it wasn't about ninja stuff. But that all ended when she turned out to be a spy for the bad guys. She had been lying to me since the first week of school, pretending to be one of my ninjas.

    The real bummer though? Naomi might've been playing for the wrong team at the moment, but I still missed her as a friend. Sure, she might've been playing me from the start, but I know that we had some real laughs together. Oh well... as my dad would say, "Such is life."

15

When I got to the trashcan, I tipped my plastic tray and banged it against the side of the plastic barrel. I watched all my food plop down into the depths of nastiness with a gross "*SPLORT*" sound.

"Seriously?" a boy said from behind me. "You hardly ate any of that food! You're just gonna waste it like that? Why even bother getting breakfast if all you're gonna do is take a bite and throw the rest out?"

The boy's name was Jesse, and he was a volunteer cashier for the kitchen. Sixth graders were allowed to volunteer for random positions like that if their grades were good enough.

"Sorry, man," I said, feeling guilty that I had just thrown out a bunch of uneaten food. The food that *I* had bought was already digesting in my belly. Jesse was talking about the two biscuits that had been thrown at me.

Jesse shook his head. "No, I'm sorry," he said, nudging me aside as he grabbed the sides of the black garbage bag that lined the barrel. "Maybe next time, *don't* buy more than one biscuit."

I didn't feel like arguing. "Right-o, captain."

He looked at me, annoyed. And then got back to pulling the garbage bag from the trashcan.

I set my tray on the kitchen counter, and headed for the lobby of Buchanan School. With only a few minutes until the start of school, I had some time to try and find my friends.

Monday. 7:35 AM. The lobby.

Out in the lobby, kids were pushing themselves through the front doors, trying to escape the freezing cold weather outside. The temperatures had dropped over the weekend, which meant it was officially time for snowballs and snow coats.

A bunch of kids were clumped together just inside the building, staring up at the newest edition of Buchanan School's list of strange things.

Right in the middle of the lobby, and the first thing anyone was going to see when walking into the school, was the brand new statue of James Buchanan, fifteenth president of the United States. The school staff had it set up over the weekend when nobody was around.

But this statue was not like any other statue. Most statues of presidents were of the man posing like someone was about to take his picture. I mean, even the most casual poses of presidential statues had the man standing in uniform, studying a map or something.

Well, the statue that Buchanan School got was completely different from those other ones.

The rumor, spreading across the earballs of everyone in

17

school, was that a video game company had gone out of business, and had sold everything in their studio for super cheap, including ginormous statues of heroes from their game.

Buchanan School bought one of the statues, and simply replaced the head of the video game character with the head of James Buchanan. It was cheaper, and much quicker for the school to do it like that.

It also meant our statue was a super *jacked* version of James Buchanan standing next to a roaring grizzly bear. And when I say "super jacked," I mean this president was *ripped*. Comic book superheroes looked *tiny* compared to this version of Buchanan!

The president wore a simple outfit sculpted to look like a fur loincloth. In his hand was a tiny pole with a tiny school flag on it, but you could totally tell that the original statue was carrying a torch or something.

"James Buchanan looks like a dude who knew how to party," Zoe's voice came from my side. "Or fight off an army of the undead. Either-or."

18

Zoe was my cousin. She was also the president of the school.

"Right?" I said, admiring the statue that stood over eight feet high. "Is he supposed to be fighting that bear, or is that bear his pet?"

"I think it's his pet," Zoe replied. "Because it looks like they're both looking at the same thing. That bear looks *angry*."

Another girl's voice came from my other side. "What a goofy thing to have in our lobby," she said.

It was Faith, another one of my good friends, who happened to also be the white ninja. It took me a long time to figure it out, but I did! Too bad anytime I tried bringing it up in conversation, she completely ignored me as if I wasn't even there.

"So..." I said, "Learn any cool ninja moves lately?"

Faith's face didn't flinch. She pressed her lips together and spoke. "That bear is freakin' me out, man."

See? She totes ignored me.

"Is it the hairstyle on the bear?" Faith asked. "It looks like someone gave it an emo haircut." Then she leaned forward and yelled. "Get a haircut, ya yak!"

"That's a bear," I said. "Not a yak."

Faith rubbed the bridge of her nose. "I know, dude. It

was a joke."

"Well, it wasn't very funny!" I said playfully. "How do you think that makes yaks feel when you confuse bears for them?"

"Dude," Faith sighed. "Yaks don't care."

"They don't care?" I said. "That's re*donk*ulous! Of course they care!"

"Quit makin' up words, Cooper!" Faith snipped.

Zoe finally leaned over. "Children," she scolded. "Maybe try using your inside voices? And what's all this talk about donkey lips?"

"Re-*donk*-u-lous," I said slowly. "Not donkey lips."

"Why're you makin' up words?" Zoe said, annoyed.

"Forget it," I groaned.

That's when Faith started bouncing her shoulders to a beat.

My cousin stared me right in the eye as her shoulders started to bounce too. Then, with her lips pressed tight… she started beat boxing.

Faith acted like she was in some sort of rap battle to save the world. "Yak, yak, yak, yak, yakkity yak, yak. Attack of the wacky yak, wacky tacky yakky yak. The yak shack! Severe lack of yak back! Yo, that yak is whack, Jack! Yak is the brand new black, mack! We're the yak pack!"

Zoe and Faith both crossed their arms at me when they were finished. I wasn't sure what to think.

"Did you guys plan on doing that or something?" I asked, totally confused. "Is that why you made the joke about the yak? So that you could break into a rap and have it not come from outer space?"

Faith giggled. "Totes," she said. "It was Zoe's idea. She wanted to work on a pretend rap over the weekend so that we could bust a rhyme outta nowhere. Next, we're gonna be able to slide into a smooth breakdance at the drop of a dime."

"It's gonna be suh-weeeeeeeeet!" Zoe said while shutting her eyes.

Man, I wasn't sure exactly what was happening, but I can't say it *wasn't* awesome. It was possible that my cousin was going to grow up stranger than me.

Zoe turned, and got serious. "So you know we've got that meeting in a few minutes, right? You didn't forget, did you?"

"No way, dude!" I said. "I didn't forget at all!"

"Cool," Zoe said. "Wait, you're not doing that thing where you say, 'no way, dude,' just to make me happy because you actually really did forget about the meeting?"

"No!" I said, again. "Way, dude!"

"He forgot," Faith joked.

With her finger, Zoe jabbed at my chest. "Ninjas. Don't. Forget."

"Sure, they do!" I said. "You're thinking of elephants! And, like, people with grudges. And also the people you owe money."

I could tell that Zoe was serious. She was pretty stressed, and after everything that she had been through, I felt bad for giving her a hard time. She had enough to worry about, and I didn't need to add to her list.

In fact, I was probably going to leave her alone for most of the week. When Zoe's got a lot on her plate, it's best to steer clear of her until *she* came looking for *you*.

Zoe slapped my book bag. "Alright, then. Good talk," she said. "See ya in a few minutes." And then her voice turned all dark. *"Don't forget!"*

"OMG, I won't!" I said.

Faith pointed at me with her finger, and wheezed, *"Don't forget, Chase Coooooooper."*

"It sounds like you're telling me not to forget about Chase Cooper," I joked.

Faith's eyes darted back and forth. She ignored my comment, and wheezed again. *"Cooooooooper..."*

After that, Zoe and Faith walked farther down the hall, disappearing in the unending sea of students rushing to their homerooms.

Glancing at the clock above the cafeteria doors, I saw that I didn't have any more time to get to my locker before school started. No bigs. I could hit it later.

I turned on the ball of my foot, and made my way through the other students gathered in the lobby that were admiring the super buff version of President Buchanan.

Brayden was right outside the crowd, standing with Slug and Gidget, waiting for me. Those three kids were the only ones in my ninja clan anymore, and I wouldn't have it any other way. I'd take a smaller ninja clan over a bigger one any day.

SLUG GIDGET BRAYDEN

"Yo," Brayden said, tilting his head. Brayden was another one of my best friends. I met him during my first week at Buchanan, and have been close ever since. He was a member of my ninja clan, and an important one too.

I knew he had my back no matter what. Like, if aliens ever invaded the planet, Brayden and I would roam the country as a team, trying to take it back from them.

Gidget had her phone pointed at the statue behind me. She snapped a photo and started tapping on the screen with her thumbs.

Slug was standing around with his hands stuffed into his pockets and his elbows locked. His head was torqued back, and his eyes were shut. I couldn't tell if he was sleeping or just giving his eyes a break.

Gidget and Slug were twins, but obviously not identical since she was a girl and he was a boy.

"What's the plan for today, boss?" Gidget asked like she didn't care, typing away on her cellphone.

"No plan," I said. "I'm thinking about laying low this week. The last month of school has been the worst. It'll be nice to take a break, y'know?"

Slug raised his eyebrows. I guess he *wasn't* sleeping. "Welllllll," he said. "It's only Monday. There's plenty of time for things to go south."

"Always the *pessimist*," Gidget said.

"Am not!" Slug said defensively. "Unless *pessimist* is a good thing? What's it mean?"

Gidget rolled her eyes. "It means you always think the worst is going to happen."

"Nuh-uh!" Slug said, and then paused. "You're talking about that meteor that's supposed to pass by the Earth at the end of the year? If it's *pessimist* for me to buy a bunch of canned goods and bottled water because the giant space boulder might destroy all of mankind, then alright, maybe I'm being *pessimist!*"

"Pessimis*tic*," Gidget said, correcting her brother. "You're not even saying the word right."

"That's because I just learned it!" Slug said. "But y'know what? I'm actually the opposite of whatever that is because I believe *dying* when a meteor hits is probably the *best* thing that can happen because all the survivors will be dealing with mutants and zombie and, like, killer robots and other junk!"

"*Optimist*," Gidget said. "The opposite of *pessimist* is *optimist*."

Slug groaned. "Stop schooling me before school, Gidget. Mom told you not to do that."

"Mom's not here," Gidget replied.

Slug made a funny face, raising his eyebrows and leaning his head over. "Then I'll *tell* on you."

Finally, Brayden put an end to the whole thing. "Guys," he said, shocked. "Seriously, you two are acting like brother and sister!"

Gidget and Slug both stared at Brayden, like, "Duh!"

"Oh, right," Brayden said. "Twins."

I pointed at the statue and changed to subject so Gidget and Slug would stop arguing with each other. "So this?" I said. "This is pretty sweet, huh?"

Gidget looked up, shielding her eyes from the fluorescent lights above. "Was President Buchanan a secret superhero?"

"Only in my dreams," I joked. This one time, I had a dream where James Buchanan visited me and helped me figure out some stuff that was going down in the school. He wasn't really a superhero in the dream, but he was still pretty helpful.

"You dream of James Buchanan?" Slug asked.

"Yes!" I said. "I mean, no. I mean, nevermind. It's a long story and I don't wanna talk about it."

"Really?" Gidget said. "Because that's *all* I wanna talk about now."

"Whatever, man," Slug groaned. He tapped at the statue in front of us. "Dude was buff, that's for sure."

"It's not really how he looked," Brayden said. "Plus I don't think he had a pet bear that followed him around."

"No?" Slug said. "Because the giant eight-foot-tall stone statue in front of us says differently."

"Look at the neck," I said. "See that line?"

Slug and Gidget both squinted at the statue.

"You can tell the body was from somewhere else," I said. "They only attached the head afterward."

"Whoa," Slug said. "He's like some kind of monster or something then… wait—"

"Don't say it," Gidget said as she dropped her head. Slug was about to say something re*donk*ulous, and she already knew it.

"What if this *was* how Buchanan really looked?" Slug suggested. "What if all the other statues and paintings of him got it wrong? What if he was really some kind of super freaky monster that had a head transplant? I mean, of course it would've been *after* he was the president, but still!"

Brayden stared at Slug. I couldn't tell if he liked the theory or not.

"So much awesome in that idea," Brayden said.

Yup. He totes agreed with Slug.

"I bet the president used his power to force a mad scientist to perform the operation," Brayden said, continuing the stream of "crazy" that had started with Slug. "He did it so he could live forever!"

"Oh!" Slug said, struck with an idea. "And that bear is the mad scientist! Like, after Buchanan got his monster jacked body, the scientist put his own brain into the bear's head!"

"The scientist… put his own brain into the bear's head?" I asked. "Like, the scientist performed that kind of operation… on himself?"

"Duh," Slug said. "Anyone who could successfully

24

transplant a human head could easily put their own brain into something else."

Gidget burst out laughing. "Do you guys hear what you're saying? Are you for real right now?"

But Brayden and Slug ignored her.

"And then they fought crime after midnight!" Brayden said.

"Of course they did," Slug said. "What else would they do?"

Gidget shook her head. I'm not sure why she was surprised at what Brayden and Slug were saying. I definitely wasn't.

"Heads up," Brayden said as his face turned serious. "Trouble at two-o-clock."

"Two-o-clock?" Slug questioned. "What happens at two? That's right before school lets out! I'm not the kind of kid who cries in front of people, but if I'm forced to stay here after school's dismissed, I just might!"

"No, dude," Brayden sighed. "I meant two-o-clock, like the direction."

"Huh?" Slug said, spinning in a circle.

Gidget groaned, slipped her cell phone back into her front pocket, and grabbed her twin brother's shoulders, pointing him in the direction that Brayden was talking about.

On the other side of the statue, and walking toward us, was Naomi. My ninja clan knew all about what happened between Naomi and me. I think even Faith knew, but Zoe was clueless. She had no idea what was going on with Naomi or The Scavengers, and I hoped to keep it that way. The less my cousin knew, the better.

Naomi and I haven't spoken a word to each other since everything went down. Wait, that's not true. She *did* tell me that the leader of The Scavengers had it out for me.

Allow me to explain who The Scavengers are. They're a group of students that collect every tidbit of information on every kid at the school.

You know that note from your BFF that you tossed in the trash during homeroom? The Scavengers picked it up. What about the conversation about the girl you have a crush on? A Scavenger overheard it. And how about the breakup note you got? Yup... it doesn't matter how many times you tore it in half, The Scavengers taped it back together.

The Scavengers were bad kids, and turned out to be a much larger club than I thought. Naomi was their leader, but that was just for the *sixth grade* Scavengers. There were seventh, and eight grade Scavengers too. And at the very top of the pyramid was a kid named Victor.

I've never met Victor before, and I wanted to keep it that way, but in a building filled with middle-school students, we were bound to run into each other at some point. I don't know what he had planned for me, but I knew it couldn't be good.

So far I've kept The Scavengers a secret from Zoe because I knew she would stress out if she knew they existed, but I've told the others in my ninja clan about them because it might be something they'd have to deal with one of these days.

A few weeks back, they had almost defeated me. I was on the edge of sacrificing my secret of being a ninja so the school would learn that The Scavengers were the real deal. Thankfully, I was saved at the last second, and didn't have to give up my ninja lifestyle.

VICTOR
CHARACTER LOCKED!
BECAUSE I'VE NEVER
ACTUALLY SEEN
HIS FACE.

"Have they tried talking to you again?" Brayden asked. "The Scavengers, I mean."

"No," I said, then I made the joke, "But I *wish* they would. It's like waiting for someone to make a move in checkers – just go already! Am I right?"

Brayden nodded, staring off into space like he was thinking about something else.

"Hey," Naomi said as she walked by.

I smiled one of those "reflex" smiles that happens when someone says hi.

Right as Naomi walked by, Wyatt passed, walking the opposite direction. I expected him to say something mean, but he didn't.

Wyatt could be considered my "Lex Luthor." He was the leader of the red ninja clan, and had been nothing but a fly in my soup since the beginning of the year. If something evil was being cooked up, you'd better believe he was the chef.

But the strange thing about Wyatt that morning was that he didn't even notice I was there. Usually, he'd walk by and flip out an insult or two, but he didn't say a thing that time.

I'm not sure why I did it, but I spoke to him. "Hey!" I said. "What gives?"

Why did I do that? He would've just walked by and everything would've been cool!

Wyatt turned his head toward me, and stared confused, like he wasn't even sure who I was. His eyes darted back and forth like he was expecting a trap to set loose on him.

Then he just *walked away!*

"That was weird," Gidget said.

"Yeah," I replied. "Why didn't he say anything?"

Gidget jabbed my arm. "No," she said angrily. "It was weird that *you* even said anything to him to begin with! You *want* him to mess with you?"

Brayden and Slug laughed.

After we said our goodbyes, I headed down the hall by myself. Most of the other kids in school were already in their homerooms. The times I was alone in the calm hallways of the school were always my favorite parts of the day. All I could hear were my jeans rubbing together and my sneakers shuffling on the tight carpet underneath.

Even though the bell had already rung, I wasn't late to homeroom since homeroom wasn't where I was going.

Zoe reminded me that I had a meeting to attend, and it was one that I wouldn't miss for the world.

Monday. 7:46 AM. The student council headquarters.

About a minute later, I was walking through the door to the student council headquarters, which was just one of the home economics classrooms at one end of the school. It was one of the only rooms that didn't have a class in it during homeroom. Zoe just called it the student council headquarters because it sounded better.

The classroom had four islands across the floor, each with six stools surrounding it, and a sink on one end. The stools were about four feet high so if you sat on one, your knees would hit the edge of the countertop. I always felt like I was too high up whenever I sat on one.

Zoe was leaning against the counter of the island that was closest to the door. The other three members of student council were on stools on the other three sides of the island, scribbling notes on stacks of white paper. It was Dani, Colin, and Bounty.

Principal Davis was even there, standing against one of the other islands in the room.

"Okay," my cousin said, glancing at me as I took a seat on one of the stools behind her. "So we've got an ice cream guy, a pizza guy, a weird pretzel guy named Teddy, a funnel

29

cake guy, and a guy who specializes in frying any kind of junk food you bring him. Are we good with food then?"

"I think so," Dani said. "Those vendors will be here to set up after school on Friday. We still haven't officially heard back from the pretzel guy, but I guess his brother goes to school here, so I can talk to him during lunch or something."

"Cool beans," Zoe said, and then she pointed at Bounty. "Where are we with the games?"

Bounty tapped his pencil, but stuttered something nobody really understood.

"Dude," Zoe said with a chill voice. She always used a calm tone when she was about to scold someone. "The Buchanan Bash is *this* Friday after school. You knew this a couple weeks ago, and had plenty of time to plan. Please tell me you didn't drop the ball on this, because it would literally *stop* my heart if you did. Is *that* what you want, Bounty? Do you want me to *die?*"

Bounty couldn't hold it in anymore and laughed. "No, I'm kidding! We're good. All the games are good to go for Friday. We have most of the stuff for all the games in the storage garage behind Buchanan. All we need are parents to volunteer to run them."

"Are you sure having a *'fun night'* isn't something just for first graders?" Colin moaned.

"It's not a *'fun night,'* it's the Buchanan Bash," Zoe explained. "I'm not about to let my presidency be a lame and boring one. The sixth graders have been through way too much at this school to not give them a huge party like this. So what if the idea of a 'fun night' is something for elementary school, you know you're gonna love it, and what's not to love? Games? Prizes? Music? Junk food? This bash is gonna rock our faces off! At the end of the night, we'll all be confused about who anyone is because our faces will have melted off by then, and— nope, y'know what? Too far. Melting faces was too far."

Everyone in the room laughed, including Principal Davis.

Zoe turned to me. "How about you, Chase? How's your thing coming along?"

"Good! It's good!" I said.

My cousin was talking about the project I had taken on for the Buchanan Bash. I thought it'd be super rad if I built a

30

giant welcome entrance that would be right inside the lobby, next to the body builder James Buchanan.

I spent most of the weekend building the main part of it, but was going to use the rest of the week to detail it. My dad helped me bring it to school earlier in the morning, and at that moment, it was sitting in the storage garage that Bounty had talked about earlier, but Zoe didn't know that.

Zoe's face beamed with a smile. "Well, where is it? I wanna see!"

I shook my head. "Nope," I said. "It's not done yet! I said you can see it when it's *done!*"

"Okay," Zoe said, "but you know that the Bash is in five days, right? Like, your thing needs to be done *before* the end of the week."

"Yeeessss," I drawled, rolling my eyes and bobbing my head back and forth. "I know when it's gotta be finished."

My cousin nodded. "Okay," she said again, "Because I know how you misunderstand things sometimes."

"No, I don't!" I said defensively. "Oh, you're talking about that *one* time, aren't you? That *one* time I got all upset because I showed up to one of your little parties that was supposed to have *free chocolate*, but you didn't have any chocolate at all?"

"Uh, yeah," Zoe said. "That party was a *chocolate-free* party, and *wasn't* a party! My mom said there was some chocolate-free chocolate cake waiting for me at home, and you overheard it, thinking a bunch of people were coming over!"

"A chocolate-free chocolate cake?" Dani asked. "How's that work?"

"It's a bunch of smooshed up garbanzo beans and soy," I said. "And honestly wasn't half that bad."

Principal Davis spoke from his side of the room. "Chase is doing a fine job with it, Zoe. You have nothing to worry about. In fact, I'm so confident that you'll love it so much that we'll unveil it to the entire school on Friday morning during the assembly for the Bash. Right there in the cafeteria."

"Seriously?" I asked, feeling my blood pump faster.

"Seriously," Principal Davis repeated.

Zoe sighed. "Anywaaaaays," she sang. "As long as you—"

Right at that second, the door to the home economics class flipped open, swinging out wide and then slamming

31

against the counter behind it. Jesse, the kitchen volunteer, stood there with sweat on his brow and grease on his sleeves.

"Principal Davis!" he shrieked as he leaned into the room. "Come quick! There's been an *incident!*"

Everyone in the room gasped. Zoe even choked on some spit. She clutched at her chest and coughed loudly.

"An incident?" Principal Davis said, concerned.

"Yes!" Jesse continued. "An incident so epic that our hearts will bleed! Someone's taken the head of James Buchanan!"

I looked at Zoe, who looked at me, and then the rest of the student council.

"Wait, wait, wait," Principal Davis said, patting at the air in front of him. "Was anyone actually hurt?"

Jesse grew frustrated. "Yes, Mr. Davis! Our *feelings* were hurt by this horrible, awful crime!"

The principal let his body rest against the counter,

breathing a sigh of relief. "Alrighty then, nobody *actually* got hurt. I swear the kids at this school are going to give me a heart attack someday."

Monday. 8:15 AM. The lobby.

Everyone in the student council, plus Jesse and I, followed Principal Davis back to the lobby of the school. The hallways weren't so calm and quiet with seven people jogging to the scene of a crime.

Jesse was telling the truth, not like we didn't believe him. The new statue of Buchanan was now headless in the lobby, which only made it more obvious that the body of the statue was from some crazy fantasy video game.

"His *head* fell off!" Bounty joked.

Principal Davis stood, silently studying the broken statue of the fifteenth president of the United States. He was staring at the spot where the head had been cracked off.

"Look at the floor," I said, pointing around my shoes. "There's some white dust where the head must've landed, but… obviously it's gone."

"This is bad," Zoe said. "The Bash is on Friday. Parents are going to come with their kids, and when they see this, it'll be an embarrassment."

Principal Davis finally spoke. "There's no way we can get a replacement head for the statue in five days. It took *months* to get the last one."

After some more grumbling, Principal Davis retreated into the front offices saying something about having to make some phone calls and how he'd rather be on a beach in Hawaii "swimmin' it up."

Bounty, Dani, and Colin continued to study the powder on the floor and give their two cents about the whole thing to each other. I took a seat on one of the benches by the front entrance to the school.

Zoe sat next to me. "What do your ninja eyes see?" she joked.

"I see a headless horseman, but with a bear instead of a horse," I answered.

"Who would do such an awful thing?" Zoe asked. "Pranks like this are so lame."

I shrugged my shoulders. "Maybe it was just an accident."

"Riiiiight," Zoe said. "Like *anything* at this school is ever *just* an accident. This school is cursed, and I bet in a hundred years when our great-great-grandkids go here, they'll be dealing with their own set of crazy problems like this."

"You think our great-great-grandkids will go to this school?" I said, excited at the thought.

"Sure, why not?" Zoe said nonchalantly.

"You think this will even be a school still? In the year 2099?" I asked.

"This was a school a hundred years ago, why wouldn't it be a school in another hundo?" Zoe said.

I scratched the back of my neck. "I should start leaving little clues around the building for my great-great-grandkid to find," I said. "How *amazing* would that be? Like, I can send him messages from the past!"

Zoe gave me the look that meant she was wondering if my descent into insanity had finally taken a turn for the worse.

"What?" I laughed. "I'm just sayin' that if I had to go around finding a bunch of stuff from our dead great-great-grandparents, it would rock my socks off!"

"Such a weirdo sometimes," Zoe grinned with a half smile. "You think you're gonna look into this prank then? The case of the missing head?"

I raised my right leg, and crossed it over my left, thinking about what it would mean if I were to investigate like I normally did. With the Bash only a few days away, I didn't have much time to run around the halls questioning kids about stuff since I still had my project to finish up.

And it sure didn't seem like the prank had anything to do with my ninja clan, so I felt like things were safe there too. Best to keep things normal rather than stir up trouble where there wasn't any.

"Nah," I said at last. "I think this is one I can pass on. A kid needs a break every now and then, right? Besides, I think Davis has it under control."

"Good," Zoe said. "For the record, I'm glad you're letting the adults handle this. I think it's time for you to just start enjoying sixth grade like a normal eleven-year-old student."

Yup, that was me... a *normal* eleven-year-old student.

Monday. 11:30 AM. Lunch.

The rest of the morning went, as swimmers would say, swimmingly. Or maybe fish would say that. But do fish know that they're swimming? Oh, man… *do fish know that they're swimming?* That question's gonna bug me for the rest of my life.

Almost all of the sixth graders were upset by the fact that someone had stolen the head of Buchanan. It didn't surprise me because even though the statue was pretty goofy looking, it was still *our* statue. It was totally lame that someone would pull a prank like that on something that sits right in the lobby of our school.

I was standing in the lunch line, waiting for my turn to pay for the pile of stuff on my tray that the school called "food." Seriously, Salisbury steak is just random chunks of meat smooshed together and slathered in gravy, resting on the soft bed of a piece of white bread. The only reason why the bread was soft was because it had been drowned in brown gravy that *might* or *might not* be mud from the soccer field. Mud with *lots* of salt and pepper.

Jesse was working the register when I got to the front of the line. He was wearing an apron that had a button on it that

37

said, "Ask me about our tomatoes."

"What about your tomatoes?" I asked, handing Jesse a dollar fifty to pay for my lunch.

"I wish people would stop asking me that," Jesse sighed as he jabbed at some of the buttons on the register. "Seriously, kids ask me that *every single day*, and it's getting on my nerves."

"Maybe stop wearing the button?" I suggested.

Jesse fiddled some more with the register, looking around like he was nervous or something.

"Oh, dude," I said, feeling bad. "I don't really care about your tomatoes. It was just a joke."

The lights on the cash register blipped, and then displayed "FREE LUNCH" on the small screen at the top.

Jesse groaned, tilting his head back.

"Free lunch?" I said.

"This register's been acting like this all day," Jesse said. "It's some kind of glitch that keeps ringing up free lunches." He slammed his fist on top of the machine. "Bad register! No! Bad!"

"Sweet!" I said. "Can I get my money back?"

Jesse sarcastically chortled. "Um, no. Lunch still needs to be paid for," he said as he reached into his apron pocket. He pulled out a rectangular slip of purple paper and set it in one of the slots inside the cash drawer, right on top of several dozen other slips of purple paper. "I gotta put one of these in each time the register glitches like this. Y'know, to keep track of how many times it's happened."

"Right," I said, looking at the cash drawer full of purple paper. Then I noticed the end of Jesse's sleeves. They were stretched out and stained with black. It had to have been from how much money he handled. I know that the bottom of my piggy bank (that's actually a zombie bank) was always caked with black dirt.

I didn't say anything else to Jesse after that. I just nodded, and took my tray of food out of the kitchen.

Monday. 11:35 AM. The cafeteria.

After leaving the cafeteria, I found Gidget and Slug sitting at a table near the front exit. Brayden wasn't there though. He was still probably in line getting his meal.

"How's your project coming along?" Slug asked, shoveling a scoop of meat and gravy into his mouth.

"There's still a lot to do with it," I said. "But I've got plenty of time before the Bash on Friday."

"You've got the whole thing built," Gidget said. All she had in front of her was an orange juice and a carton of fries. "All you really need to do is add the finishing touches, right?"

"Right," I said. "Some paint and extra little things to glue onto it."

"What is it again?" Slug asked before shoveling another huge bite of food into his mouth. He had just about cleared his tray of food in the last twenty seconds.

"It's just an entryway," I explained. "It'll stand in the lobby, next to the statue of Buchanan, who will hopefully find his head by then." Something in my brain clicked. "Ohhhhh, *that's* why my mom always tells me that I'd lose my own head if it wasn't attached! I get it now!"

"You didn't get that before?" Gidget asked, crunching

40

down on a French fry.

"No, I guess I never really thought of it," I said. "So the entryway is going to look like you're walking into a crazy looking circus with fake robots and electronics and tubing. It's gonna be all junky science fiction stuff."

"Sounds cool," Gidget said. "But why?"

"Because why not?" I asked. "Zoe's all about presentation, and I thought it'd be pretty cool if that was the first thing kids saw when walking through the doors on Friday night."

"Makes sense," Gidget said, but I wasn't sure if she was actually paying attention. She was back to tapping the screen of her cell phone on the table.

"So hey," Slug said nervously. "I was thinking…"

Gidget looked up from her phone. "Does it hurt?" she asked, and then clenched her fist, whispering to herself. "Oh, burn! Easy, Gidget, don't celebrate yet. Wait until he's

41

begging for mercy. Only then can you gloat. That's just good sportsmanship."

For a second, I thought Slug was going to be serious, but... he wasn't.

"Giraffes?" Slug said, tilting his head. "Too tall? Or not tall enough?"

"What kind of question is that?" his sister asked.

"The kind of question that a scientist asks," Slug said, annoyed. "How do you think scientists get so smart? It's because they ask whatever question is on their mind."

"But their questions aren't about giraffes being too tall," Gidget said.

"Wait," I said. "Slug might be onto something here."

"Seriously?" Gidget sighed.

"Are giraffes just horses with super long necks?" I asked, looking at Slug.

"No," Gidget said, letting her phone drop to the table.

"And if they are, then why do *they* get the long necks?" I continued.

"Could you ride a giraffe?" Slug said.

I shrugged my shoulders, looking at Gidget.

She pouted, raising her eyebrows. "Y'know," she said honestly. "That's a good question. I don't think so... but... I don't know."

"See?" Slug said, sitting back and crossing his arms. "I'm askin' all the important things over here."

"Can you imagine if a country rode an army of giraffes into battle?" Gidget said.

I tried to see something like that in my head. "It would be the funniest thing ever, or the most terrifying thing ever. Either way, the army *without* the giraffes would lose."

"Dude," Slug said, super seriously and leaning closer to me. He had the most intense look in his eyes. "What if the army riding the giraffes... was a *ninja* army?"

I laughed, imagining a bunch of ninjas riding on the backs of giraffes.

"This just in," I said, making my best radio DJ voice. "That idea is awesome sauce."

"You should put robot giraffes on your entryway," Slug suggested. "That would be a small detail that takes the whole thing to the next level, y'know? Epic."

For a moment, I considered it, but then shook the idea

out of my head because of how much work it would mean for me. "Nope," I said. "Besides, Brayden might be upset if I changed anything about it."

"Why?" Gidget asked.

"Because he helped me with it over the weekend," I said, looking over the lunchroom to see if my friend had gotten lost. "Speaking of Brayden, have you guys seen him yet?"

As if to answer my question, Gidget gasped. A split-second later, I heard some other kids in the lunchroom do the same. Everyone was looking out of the tinted glass windows next to the table my friends and I were sitting at.

Outside in the lobby, I saw Brayden, but he wasn't alone. His head was down as he walked slowly in front of two hall monitors wearing suits that they probably didn't need to be wearing.

Following behind all three of them was Principal Davis carrying a white stone object that looked familiar.

It was part of the head from the James Buchanan – the hairpiece.

"Whaaaat?" I whispered.

"Did *Brayden* take the head?" Slug asked.

"No way," I said. "There's no way!"

"It's not the whole head though," Gidget said, pressing her face against the glass wall of the cafeteria, staring out the window. "It's just the hair. It looks like the rest broke off or something."

Brayden stopped at the front door of the office and turned. His eyes met mine, and he shook his head with barely any movement. It was his ninja way of telling me he didn't do it. Okay, it wasn't really a *ninja* way of telling me, but that just sounded way cooler.

Principal Davis was the last to walk into the front offices, shutting the door behind him. Through the frosted glass windows of the office, I watched as the four blurry figures marched to the back section and disappeared.

"Bummer," Slug said. "Just when ya think ya know a guy."

"He didn't do it," I said. "He *wouldn't* have done something like that. I've known him for—"

"A few months," Gidget said, interrupting me.

I paused, nodding. "A few months, but that's more than enough time to get to know a guy, and I know that Brayden would never ever do a thing like this."

Some kids walked into the cafeteria from the lobby, already in conversation.

"Someone said they saw it fall out of Brayden's book bag!"

"He's so busted, and good thing too, because that's just wrong – taking the head of a statue like that."

"Yeah, what'd he think was gonna happen? What a nimrod. This'll go on his permanent record, for sure."

"You know permanent records aren't a real thing, right? They just tell you they're real so you'll fall in line."

"Get outta here with you and your conspiracy theories!"

Gidget looked up from her phone. "It fell out of his book bag?"

"He was set up," I said confidently. "That's the only answer that makes sense."

"I don't know..." Gidget said quietly.

After seeing Brayden disappear into the front offices, I had lost my appetite. Slug gladly took the rest of my food and disposed of it into his own belly.

The kids in the cafeteria were in full gossip mode, sharing their own thoughts and feelings about Brayden stealing the head of the statue. It was hard to listen to, so after Slug finished slurping down my food, we headed into the lobby to get away from the noise.

Monday. 11:55 AM. The lobby.

The lobby wasn't much quieter than the cafeteria. There were students out by the statue, shocked about how Brayden had the ability to do such an awful thing.

I stared at the spot on the statue where James Buchanan's head should've been. Was it possible that Brayden *was* the thief? Was I being too hopeful that one of my best friends wasn't capable of such an act? I didn't see him before school started that morning, so maybe...

And then I spotted Wyatt nestled away in the corner of the nook by the front entrance of the school. He was on the carpet, with his knees up, chewing on his fingernails. He kept looking back and forth over his shoulder, like he was afraid something was going to jump out and get him.

Of course Wyatt was out there. He *had* to have something to do with Brayden and the missing head of James Buchanan!

I decided there wouldn't be a better time to talk to Wyatt, so I marched up to him.

"What's your game this time?" I said to Wyatt.

I'm not sure that Wyatt even noticed me. He was too busy gnawing on his fingers. The nails that I could see had

46

been chewed down so far that they looked raw. Sick.

Wyatt looked up at me without turning his head, moving only his eyeballs. When he noticed it was me, he jumped to his feet, and stuffed his hands into his pockets. "What do *you* want?"

"I *said*—" but couldn't finish my sentence because Wyatt's attention snapped to his left, and then he shuffled away from me, jogging down the hall to the right.

"So that was odd," Gidget said behind me. "Even for Wyatt."

It was only a few days ago that I saw Wyatt talking to Naomi. I was so sure that they would join forces to try and destroy me once and for all, but after seeing how distracted Wyatt was that morning, and how he just ran away, I was beginning to doubt their team up.

Something was off about Wyatt. That much was for sure. Maybe he cracked after Naomi told him about The Scavengers. Maybe he was spooked because he knew they were real now?

"Hasn't Brayden been framed for something before?" Slug asked, staring at the buff statue in front of us.

"No, not really," I said. "Back at the beginning of the year, he got caught once trying to help, but ended up getting in trouble for that."

"So you think you're gonna look into this prank then?" Gidget asked, using the same exact words that my cousin did, not even four hours earlier.

But this time, I didn't even need to think about my answer. Brayden was a friend, and he needed my help. "Of course I am," I said, and then faced Gidget and Slug. " I mean, of course *we* are."

The twins both smiled at me, ready for the adventure that was waiting for us.

After another moment of joking around, Gidget and Slug went down one of the hallways, waiting for the end of lunch. I took a spot by the corner where Wyatt had been sitting, to try and collect my thoughts.

When I first arrived to school that morning, the head of the statue was still where it belonged. Even after the first bell rang, it was there.

It wasn't until I was about twenty minutes into the student council meeting that someone pulled the prank – that's

47

when Jesse burst through the door to tell Principal Davis something was wrong.

So whatever happened, happened within the first twenty minutes of the school day, when everyone was *supposed* to be in homeroom. Nobody would've been in the cafeteria yet so there wouldn't have been any witnesses, and since the front office windows were frosted glass, there was no way anyone could've seen anything from there.

I'm not 100% sure of where Brayden was that morning, but he should've been in homeroom like everyone else.

Of course there was always Naomi or even Victor to worry about, but if they had anything to do with the prank, they probably would've contacted me by now.

Just then, a paper airplane almost poked me in the eye, scaring me enough that I jumped back and let out a tiny screech.

The airplane turned downward and darted to the floor, stopping at my feet.

I glanced around, trying to see who it was that threw the plane, but there wasn't anyone giggling the way the kids did during breakfast when they threw their biscuits at me.

Looking at my feet, I noticed some writing on the inside of the airplane. I wouldn't have thought anything of it if it weren't for the fact that it was my own name written onto the sheet of paper.

"Lovely," I sighed, picking up the plane. I was surprised at how perfectly folded the wings were. In my entire life, I've never been able to make such a flawless paper airplane.

I unfolded it carefully, the way my mom opens her presents on her birthday so she can reuse the wrapping paper.

On the inside of the plane was a short note.

Chase Cooper,
Victor would like to meet with you behind the cafeteria,
near the dumpsters.
- The Scavengers

"Oh, wonderful," I said to myself sarcastically. "More drama!"

The last time The Scavengers sent me a note, it was on fancy stationary that looked like a wedding invitation. The note I was holding was a flimsy sheet of loose leafed paper folded into an airplane. Why the huge difference, I wondered.

Crumpling the plane up in my hands, I jumped to my feet, spinning in place and shooting the ball of paper toward the nearest garbage can like I was playing basketball. It was an "over-the-top" style of throwing it away, but I wanted to be sure that whoever delivered it saw that I didn't care.

Too bad it missed the basket anyway.

"*Aiiiir ball*," I sang with a high-pitched voice as I picked it up and dropped it into the garbage. Nobody heard the joke though.

As much as I would've loved meeting Victor and dealing with The Scavengers again, which was to say I wouldn't have loved it, I had more important things to worry about – like saving Brayden from detention, suspension, or even getting expelled.

Tuesday. 7:00 AM. The lobby.

The next morning, I had my dad drop me off at school a little earlier than usual. You know I mean serious business when I wake up with enough time to actually eat breakfast at home.

The cold air was still on my clothes when I stepped through the doors of Buchanan, greeted by the headless statue of the fifteenth president of the United States.

Gidget and Slug were supposed to meet me in the lobby, but they weren't there yet. And I was pretty sure Brayden would be locked away in detention for the rest of the week. I would've talked to him, but whenever he gets detention, his parents ground him from his cellphone, the Internet, and anything else people use to communicate with the outside world.

So for a few minutes, I was going to be on my own in the lobby.

The part of the carpet that had the white powder had been vacuumed up. I knelt closer and ran my finger along the floor, scraping the carpet to see if I could make any dust pop up. It didn't work, but it didn't matter since it wasn't that important.

50

I looked up at the neck of the statue, where the head should've been. It wasn't really surprising to see that the head came off so easily. The top of the neck was perfectly flat, like the headless mannequins I see at the mall sometimes.

Leaning over the base of the statue, I reached out and tapped the foot of the bear that was next to Buchanan. The bear itself was solid rock, but the platform that held the entire statue felt pretty flimsy – not like it was going to fall over, but that it slightly rocked back and forth when I nudged it.

"Well, no wonder his head fell off," I said aloud. "The thing's a piece of junk."

At that moment, I heard the door to the front offices slam shut. I spun around, feeling my stomach drop, and expected a lecture from the principal. There was nothing wrong with what I was doing, but I still felt like I had been caught doing *something*.

Instead of Principal Davis, it was Miss Chen-Jung, the school janitor, grumbling as she pulled her cart of cleaning supplies through the door.

But if she noticed me, she didn't show it. Instead, she spoke to herself with a quick, but soft voice.

"Just see if it turns up somewhere," she said in a mocking tone. "Like someone's just gonna take it and return it like they were *borrowing* it."

She stopped in the middle of the hallway when she noticed I was there.

For a moment, we both stared at each other. I stared because I didn't know what to say. She stared because I think she was surprised to see a student in the lobby so early in the morning.

Finally, she snapped out of her trance and spoke. "What?" she asked, annoyed.

I laughed nervously, turning my eyes to the floor. "Nothing! I just... um, I just... I don't know."

"Did *you* take it?" Miss Chen-Jung asked with an evil eye.

"The head?" I asked, pointing at the statue in front of me. "Never! I'd never—"

"My printer!" Miss Chen-Jung said, cutting me off. "Davis says it'll have to wait because fixing the statue before the Bash has to come first, but my maintenance closet just got that printer over the weekend, and *already* it's been stolen!

51

Already! This school! Seriously, this school!"

After her short rant, the janitor gripped the handles of her cart and pushed it down the hall. I never know what to say to someone when they use me as a soundboard to go off on something. Lucky for me, she just walked away.

A gust of ice-cold air pushed through me, filtering through my clothes and my hair. I turned around to see Gidget and Slug walking through the front doors of the school.

"Find anything?" Gidget asked immediately.

Slug still looked half-asleep.

Gidget nodded her head at her twin brother. "He'll be like that until about nine-o-clock. His body might be awake, but his brain is still trying to switch on."

Slug's mouth dropped open slightly as he moaned, "Uh-huh..."

"I only got here a little bit ago," I said. "There's really nothing to see. The statue doesn't have a head. The neck is smooth so it probably came off pretty easily. And the base of the whole thing rocks back and forth."

Gidget pushed against the base with her foot, moving the whole thing. "Well, duh-doy. Of course the statue broke where it did. With a shaky bottom, and a head that probably wasn't attached too well, it would be easy to knock that noggin off."

Slug grunted a laugh. "Shaky bottom," he slurred with a little drool collecting at the corners of his mouth.

Gidget gave her brother an annoyed looked, and then sighed as if she were disappointed in his sense of humor.

"Hey, guys," Slug said slowly. "Guys, check this out... I had this awesome idea last night..."

Gidget and I waited for Slug to continue, but he might've fallen asleep again.

Gasping, Slug's eyes opened wide, and then fell back into the half-shut position. "We're, like, the ninjas of the school... the good guys... right? So, um, we're, like, here to *avenge* kids who are bullied and stuff..."

"No," I said. "We're *not* here to *avenge* others."

But Slug ignored what I said. That, or he didn't hear me.

"So I was thinking our ninja clan needed a name," Slug said, as if he were sleep talking. "We'll call ourselves 'The School Avengers,' but shorten the name to 'The Sc'avengers' so it's easier to say."

"Dude," Gidget said, rubbing the bridge of her nose.

"You wanna call us 'The Sc'avengers?'" I questioned, and then repeated it again so Slug could understand. "The Sc'avengers... The Scavengers... Sc'avengers. Scavengers. Dude, is this clicking at all?"

Slug nodded with a dorky smile.

"When he wakes up, he'll realize what a dumb idea it was," Gidget said.

Slug's face didn't change as he swayed back and forth.

Pulling a small notepad from my book bag, I flipped it open and went over some notes with the two members of my ninja clan. "So I wrote a short list of kids who I think might've had something to do with this. You guys know them too. We'll start with the obvious ones first, like Wyatt, Jake, Naomi, Sebastian—"

Gidget interrupted me. "Um," she hummed. "You can't *start* with anyone you want to start with. That's not fair to those kids. You actually shouldn't start with *anyone*."

"What're you talking about?" I asked. "These are the kids who have caused trouble before and—"

"But you're already looking at them like they're guilty," Gidget explained. "Again, that's not fair to them. Plus it doesn't really help our case right now. What if it *wasn't* any of those kids? Then you're just wasting time by looking in the wrong place. I mean, I know Wyatt's a bad dude, but you can't just point your finger at him and say that maybe he did it."

"But..." I stopped, surprised by what Gidget had said. She was totally and completely right about how I was trying to solve the case.

And then Gidget buttered some bread of knowledge for me. "Some people only act bad because everyone expects them to act that way. What if that's what's going on with Wyatt? Like, everyone keeps *telling* him that he's the bad guy, so he just keeps *acting* like it. What if we tried treating him like a normal dude sometime?"

"You're starting to sound like Zoe," I said, smirking.

"She's a smart kid," Gidget said. "So I'll take that as a compliment."

Miss Chen-Jung poked her head up from behind the statue. Gidget and I jumped at her sudden appearance. Slug didn't move, but that was because he was still in "hibernation" mode.

"What're you kids doing?" the janitor asked, suspicious.

Gidget pointed at the statue. "Trying to figure out what happened to the head."

"That Brayden kid took it," Miss Chen-Jung said. "Everyone knows that already, so I'll ask you again – what are you kids doing out here?"

"That's just it," I said. "We don't think Brayden's the one who took it. He's a close friend, and we know that he would never do something like that, not just because it's wrong, but because it's kind of a lame prank."

Miss Chen-Jung studied us for a moment, and then looked at the statue of James Buchanan. She was an odd duck.

"I mean, you're out here a lot, right?" I asked.

The janitor nodded, but said nothing.

"Is there anything you saw that might send us in the right direction?"

Miss Chen-Jung stood silently for a moment, and then spoke again. "I only saw the statue after the head was stolen, so I didn't actually *see* anyone take it. But… there *was* a girl out here… watching me clean up the mess from the corner back there. The only reason I noticed her was because she was there for a really long time."

"What'd she look like?" Gidget asked.

Miss Chen-Jung shrugged her shoulders. "I didn't see her face, but she had black hair."

"Great," I said. "There's about a billion of girls here with black hair."

Gidget huffed. "I don't think there's a *billion*."

"You know what I meant," I said.

I turned toward the janitor to ask her more, but she was gone – vanished without a trace, like some kind of ninja janitor that traveled between dimensions when she—no wait, she was just down the hall. She must've left when Gidget and I were talking.

I shut my notepad and stuffed it into my back pocket. "So we're dealing with a girl with black hair," I said. I wanted to bring up Naomi's name, but after everything Gidget said about not blaming someone before any evidence, I decided not to. "Then, where do we start?" I asked, stressing that the only plan I had wasn't much of a plan at all.

Gidget stretched her arm out. A cellphone slipped out of the sleeve, landing perfectly in the palm of her hand, like it was just another part of her body that she controlled by flexing different muscles.

"We'll start with a friend of mine," Gidget said, typing a text on her phone. "I got a friend who deals with these kinds of things."

"You have a friend who deals with the lost heads of statues?" I asked.

Slug groaned with his eyes half shut. I *think* it was a laugh, but his body still hadn't fully woken up yet so I wasn't sure.

"No," Gidget replied, rolling her eyes. "My friend… deals with this a lot. She deals with, like, investigations and stuff."

"Does she go here?" I asked.

Gidget nodded, finishing up her text. I head the swoosh sound of her message being sent.

"Cool," I said. "Do I know her?"

"Maybe," Gidget replied.

"Is she a sixth grader?"

"Yes."

"Do I have any classes with her?"

"I don't know," Gidget paused. "Maybe?"

"Is she short?" I asked.

"Does it matter?"

"No, but is she short?"

"Not really. She's about our height."

"Is that who you're always texting?"

"She's *one* of the people I'm always texting, yes."

"Does she know me?"

"Yes."

"Really?" I felt kind of excited. "What's she say about me?"

"Are you serious?" Gidget asked, putting a hand on her hip. "You don't even know who we're talking about and you want to know what she says about you?"

I shrugged my shoulders. "Why not?"

Gidget's phone buzzed in her hand.

"Is it her?" I asked, hopeful. "I'll call her the *informant*."

Gidget read the text on her phone, leaning away from me. "You're starting to irk me," she said. "But yes, it's her, and her *name* is K-pop. Please don't call her the informant."

"But I should call her K-pop?" I asked. "Her name is K-pop?"

"She has a thing for Korean pop music," Gidget explained, and then she snapped a picture of me with her phone. "The music flows through her veins like blood, so people call her K-pop."

"Are you sending her a picture of me?" I asked, uncomfortable because I didn't even get the chance to make a dorky face.

"Mm-hmm," Gidget hummed.

"You can't just..." I started saying, but stopped. "Is she cute?"

"Guh," Gidget groaned, rolling her eyes.

I gestured toward Gidget's phone. "What'd her text say?"

Gidget raised her phone and read her message again before answering. "K-pop said there's not much she, herself, can do for us, but she sent a message to someone named Valentine about what's going on. I guess she's setting up a meeting between the two of you."

"Brody?" I said.

"Yeah, Brody," Gidget said. Her phone buzzed again. "Oh, cool. You need to find him during lunch. He'll be up on the second floor, in room 801."

"I know Brody," I said, feeling relieved that it wasn't some new kid I had to make friends with. "Tell her to tell him I'll be there."

Gidget jabbed her brother's arm with her fist, getting him to wake up a little more. "C'mon, dude," she said, heading for the kitchen. "Let's get some *breckie* in you. That oughta wake you up."

I think *breckie* meant breakfast.

"Later, guys," I said. "I'll find you after I meet with Brody."

"You're not hungry?" Gidget asked as she guided her brother like he was some sort of sleep walking zombie.

"Not this morning," I said. "I ate at home."

After the twins disappeared through the doors of the kitchen, I took a seat on the nook, staring at the statue, hoping maybe I'd see something that I missed earlier.

I had no luck though.

The garbage can next to me was the one I had used the day before to throw away my note from The Scavengers – the one that was folded up like a paper airplane.

From where I was sitting, I could see the airplane sitting on top of a pile of crumpled candy wrappers and other junk. Miss Chen-Jung must not have emptied that trash yet.

All of a sudden, the Asian janitor reappeared out of nowhere, jumping up from behind the garbage can, scaring me half to death.

I yelped, scooting back on the carpet in the nook. *"What are you?"* I shouted. "How are you able to just appear outta nowhere?"

Miss Chen-Jung smirked at me, but didn't answer. It was the creepiest smile I'd ever seen on a janitor's face before. She went about her business and pulled the bag out of the garbage can, and along with it, my note from The Scavengers.

I tried to hide the fact that my heart was skipping beats as Miss Chen-Jung tied off the garbage bag and dropped it on top of her cart. After that, she continued down the hall, disappearing around the corner. At least, I *thought* she disappeared. She could've been standing right behind me for all I knew.

Miss Chen-Jung said she saw a girl with black hair staring at her while she cleaned up the mess left behind by the prankster.

A lot of girls at the school had black hair.

Naomi had black hair.

I don't know why Naomi would be involved with a prank like this, or what it had to do with Brayden, but as his friend, I knew I had to at least check it out. If Naomi *was* involved, then it meant Victor was too.

Victor wanted to meet with me. I already told him no, so if I were to find him now, it would be on my terms, right?

"Welp," I sighed to myself. "Looks like I'm about to meet Victor."

Tuesday. 11:30 PM. The kitchen.

The note from The Scavengers told me that Victor wanted to meet outside the cafeteria, by the dumpsters or something. I only hoped that it was a spot he visited during lunch everyday, otherwise I'd have to try to find him some other way.

At the front of the lunch line, I handed Jesse a dollar fifty, only to watch the register ring my food up as free again.

"Still broke?" I asked.

Jesse took my money, and then slipped another rectangular piece of paper into the cash drawer. "Still broke," he said, shaking his head like he was more annoyed than angry.

The air in the kitchen normally smelled of fried chicken (even when there wasn't fried chicken cooking), but that's not what my nose was picking up. There was a hint of something nasty, like chemicals or something. It reminded me of black magic markers.

"What's that smell?" I asked.

"Food," Jesse replied casually.

"No," I said. "There's something *else* though, like marker or something…?"

"Oh," Jesse said. "Yeah, I think someone's working on a sign in the back or something. I don't know for sure, but I think it's, like, for a bake sale or something."

"Oh, cool," I said.

"So, hey," he continued. "That kid who got busted yesterday... that's your friend, right?"

"Brayden?" I asked. "Yeah, why?"

Jesse fidgeted a bit before answering. "Just wondering. Is he okay?"

"I think so," I said. "Got a week in the slammer 'cause of it."

Jesse nodded. "Bummer, man."

It was nice to know that other people cared about my friends. After paying for my food, I stepped into the cafeteria, only to be greeted by a cell phone pointed at my face.

"Smile," the girl holding the phone said.

Of all the people it could've been, it was Naomi.

I wanted to ask her right there if it was her that Miss Chen-Jung had seen, but I didn't. It wasn't just because of what Gidget had said, but I thought that if Naomi somehow *was* part of it, I didn't need her knowing I suspected anything... yet.

"Please stop," I said, stepping around Naomi.

She followed me, holding her phone in her hand while pointing it at me. "Come on," she said as if we were still best friends. "I just got this new phone, and I knew you'd want to check it out! The screen is huge, and games look amazing on it!"

I didn't say anything as I took my tray and continued walking between some lunch tables.

"Chase," Naomi said, getting ahead of me. "Come on..."

I had to stop walking because she cut me off. I really didn't know what to do. I was stuck standing there with my lunch tray, in front of a girl who shattered our friendship like a broken glass.

Setting my tray down on the table beside me, I gave up and took a seat. Naomi took the spot across from mine, still pointing her cellphone at me.

"Are you recording video?" I asked.

Naomi smiled. And then she set her phone on the table. "Sorry," she said. "It's just... it's a new phone, y'know? I'm

pretty obsessed with it, filming everything like crazy. I've
never had a phone that shot in 1080p before, and I—"
    I think she could tell I wasn't interested in hearing the
specs of her phone.
    "Sorry," she said again, softer that time. "I've filmed so
much video on this thing that it probably weighs more than
your phone now."
    "That's not how digital works," I said.
    Naomi paused, and then quietly said, "I *know*... it was a
joke."

    The silence between us was awkward, but instead of
filling it with pointless words, I scarfed down all my food like
my life depended on it, which if you think about it, everyone's
life depends on them scarfing food. Right?
    "I miss you," Naomi said flatly.
    It was weird to hear her say that. I almost coughed out
all my food when she did.
    She must've understood my reaction because she
continued, "Not in a cheesy romance movie kind of way, but I

miss you as a *friend*, you dork. I thought about all the different ways to say that without sounding like a lamewad, and I couldn't think of any way that was better than just saying I miss you."

I said nothing, but it was killing me.

Naomi chuckled. "Remember that time when you spent the whole day talking like a caveman?"

Naomi was trying to pull the ol' "remember the time" trick to get me to smile.

"Oog! Chase not finish homework," Naomi said in a low voice, and with the worst impression of a caveman I've ever heard. "Ooga, oog! Chase need bathroom! Chase go number one! Maybe number two? Chase not sure until Chase go to bathroom! Wait, teacher just want Chase to find tree?"

I couldn't help it. I cracked a smile. "I only did that because I lost a bet," I said, surprised at how normal it felt to talk to Naomi. "It was either that or wear a dress to school. When my dad wins a bet, you better be sure he makes me follow through with my end of the deal."

"You got in-school detention because of that," Naomi laughed.

"Just for one period," I said. "Mrs. Olsen was pretty annoyed with me that day."

Naomi smiled at me, but didn't say anything else right away. I think she just wanted things to feel normal between us for another second.

"I know things can never be the same with us again," Naomi finally said. "But I want you to know that I'm sorry. I'm sorry about everything that happened."

I couldn't believe my ears. Naomi was apologizing for the fact that she had turned against me, and that she had turned the entire school against me. Like saying sorry was going to fix all the damage she'd done.

I really didn't feel like sitting across from her anymore because I knew that if I started flappin' my mouth, I was only going to say something I'd regret.

Besides, I still needed to get outside to see if Victor was around. Yes, I was going to speak to him about the girl who was, at that moment, sitting two feet away from me. I could've just asked Naomi, but with our history, it was too difficult.

"Okay," I said to my ex-bestie as I took my tray and got up from my spot. "You're sorry. I get it. I heard you say it."

As I walked to the trashcan, I was afraid Naomi was still following me, but when I looked over my shoulder, she wasn't. She was still at the table all by herself, staring at the spot where I had been sitting.

My insides crawled, but not in a way I thought they would. I was shocked because I wasn't happy to get away from Naomi. I was more sad that she was alone.

I shook the feeling from my gut as I emptied my tray into the trashcan.

Brody wanted me to find him during lunch, but before that, I had a couple questions I needed to ask Victor.

Tuesday. 11:40 AM. Outside by the dumpsters.

About a minute later, I was outside.

The side doors to the cafeteria were never locked, and most of the teachers were cool with kids going in and out as long as it was during lunch, and within fifty feet of the cafeteria.

It was a place where students could snack on junk and hang out with friends, but on this blistery cold day, there wasn't anyone else out there.

The dumpsters were to my right. There was a small security camera at the top of the school, pointed right down at the giant garbage containers, probably to keep kids from tagging them with spray paint.

Not that anyone would ever want to hang out by the dumpsters for longer than a couple minutes. The stench back there was awful!

Have you ever felt nervous about having to do something, and then you find out that you might *not* have to do that thing because of something else? Sometimes it's the best feeling in the world. Like, I *wanted* to talk to Victor, but I was *also* freaked out by it. So if Victor *wasn't* by the dumpsters, I would've been pretty happy about it.

But as I got closer to the spot where Victor was supposed to be, I saw a student. There was a kid sitting on one of those concrete parking stops behind the dumpsters, but it was just the one kid. There wasn't anyone else. The only other living things around the student were a bunch of birds.

I quickly scanned the area for other Scavengers, but was shocked to see there weren't any. Maybe the kid on the parking stop wasn't Victor after all.

Making a wide circle, I leaned over to get a better look at the student. I had never met Victor before so I had no idea what he looked like. All I knew was that he was an eighth grader who wore glasses.

But when I saw the front of his shirt, I knew it was him. On the left side of his chest, there was a white patch that had the name "Victor" sewn on it, with red thread.

And I was wrong about Victor being alone. He might've been the only kid out there, but he was surrounded by about a dozen pigeons. They were pecking at tiny pieces of popcorn that Victor was feeding them.

I guess the cold weather didn't bother pigeons.

Victor looked up at me, squinting because the sky behind me was so bright from the clean sun and clear skies. For an eighth grader, and the leader of The Scavengers, he wasn't too scary.

VICTOR

His hair was slicked back and he had an earing in his left ear. I hid a smile because he looked like a member of one of my mom's old boy band CDs from the '90s.

Victor exhaled through his nose slowly, pressing his lips together. "Chase Cooper," he said. "As I live and breathe."

"You must be Victor," I said.

The boy with the earing nodded, but didn't stand up. He continued to pinch popcorn pieces from the bag so he could lightly toss them out to his bird friends. "Pigeons are so rad, aren't they? Did you know they can fly almost a hundred miles an hour? And that it's believed that a pigeon might be able to see up to twenty six *miles* away?"

"Um, no," I said honestly. "I did *not* know that."

"Plus they help my stress levels," Victor said. "I feel calm when I feed them. My headaches disappear when it's just me and my birds... such *awful* headaches."

"Yeeeeah," I said, unsure of what else to say.

Victor pointed his snack toward me. "Would you like a popped bag of corn?"

"A what?" I asked. "You mean the popcorn?"

"Some people call it that," Victor said with a snide smile. "I prefer calling it a popped bag of corn."

"Yeah, *that's* not weird," I said, and then added, "And by that, I mean it's *totes* weird. How are you allowed to be out here right now? Eighth graders have lunch at a different time than the sixth graders. Shouldn't you be in class?"

"This *is* my class," Victor said.

"Feeding birds is your class?" I said, confused.

"It's my free period," he explained. "And I've chosen to sit out here and study pigeons. It's a science credit." Victor tossed a piece of popcorn to one of the birds. "You left me hangin' yesterday. I was out here waiting for you, and you just *left me hanging.*"

I looked around. "Where are the rest of your Scavengers? I thought you'd be heavily guarded since you're their leader."

"No," Victor said, shaking his head. "Not everything needs a huge scene. I just wanted to meet the kid who beat Naomi. She's my little *champion*, you know. I've never met a girl who showed more promise as a Scavenger. She'll go far in life."

I was gonna ask him about Naomi and the statue, but what he said distracted me. "Wait, you just wanted to *meet* me?"

"You've started a war, Chase, and I'm going to finish it," Victor said, looking at me through his thick-rimmed glasses. "Part of the art of war is to know yourself, and to know your enemy. Well, I know myself pretty well, and based on all the information we've gotten about you, I know you too. But I've realized that I've never *met* you, and I think it would be a mistake to not *meet* with my enemy… before I destroy him. Do you know yourself? I mean, do you really *know* yourself?"

"I had a dream where I met my evil clone on a space station…" I stopped my dumb mouth from talking. *Why would I talk about my weird dreams?*

Victor looked at me funny, but continued. "Naomi really messed up your world, didn't she?"

"You have no idea," I said.

"She's cute, right?" Victor asked. "She just got that new phone, and is filming everything like a tiny child with a brand

66

new toy." He paused. "She failed to beat you in the end though, didn't she? She got greedy, and missed the big picture. If only she had a little more focus with you…"

"What're you talkin' about?" I asked, feeling my blood boil. I was beginning to think it was a mistake to find this kid. It was a massive, *massive* mistake.

Victor cleared his throat as he kept feeding the pigeons around him. "I'm not gonna mess with your social life, Chase. I won't even make it so your friends hate you. Naomi did all that, and it was too much for her to control. In fact, I'll even give you my *word* that my plan *isn't* to make anyone hate you. No… I'm simply going to take the thing that matters the most to you."

I stared at Victor. "And what's that?"

"Your ninja clan," Victor answered coldly.

I laughed. "You think people haven't tried that already? Naomi did a bang up job when she took most of them from me. They all went and joined your little club of psychos!"

Victor stood from his spot on the parking stop. He was short. Like, super short, at least for an eight grader. "Don't forget that The Scavengers know all your secrets, including your deepest darkest struggles and fears…"

I remained silent as Victor spoke.

"I know that you've struggled with being a good leader since the start of school," Victor explained confidently. "My plan is simple – I'll take your ninja clan away from you permanently, but not in the same way Naomi did. No, your ninjas will understand that there's really no point to your clan. That there's no point to your leadership, and that you guys… just have no purpose."

I hated what Victor was saying because a small part of me was afraid he was right.

"Once your ninja clan is finished," Victor went on, "you'll have nothing to identify with. You'll be all alone in this school – the lone kid with no friends. And then you can do what you've been training to do the entire time you've been here… disappear into the shadows. Wanna know the best part about my plan? *Nobody* will even notice because *nobody* will even care."

I kept my mouth shut. This kid was so full of himself that he just told me his entire plan. The thing that scared me the most was that he was so brutally honest about it. He knew what he was going to do, and he knew there wasn't anything I could do to fight it.

"Ouch, right? Man, I'm an evil dude!" Victor said loudly, and doing the robot dance while making a beat with his mouth. "Nnn-st, nnn-st, nnn-st, nnn-st, nnn-st, nnn-st, nnn-st, nnn-st!"

I tried to say more, but Victor just kept doing the robot and making techno sounds every time I tried to speak. It was a little like Zoe and Faith when they were beatboxing. Was this something that was cool now? Was I late to the beatboxing party or something?

Backing away slowly, I waited until I could see the cafeteria doors again, and then without another word, I left the kid to dance by himself by the dumpsters.

Victor was easily one of the strangest boys I'd ever met at Buchanan. He was also one of the scariest.

Tuesday. 11:55 PM. The second floor.

Within minutes, I was on my way up the stairs to the second floor of the school. Lunch was almost over, and I'd already goofed up twice by speaking to Naomi and Victor. I should've just come to Brody right at the beginning of lunch. I probably wouldn't have felt so defeated if I had.

On the second floor, I read the numbers on each door. Most of the upstairs were science labs and storage rooms, so I wasn't sure why Brody wanted me to find him up there.

All the sixth graders were still in the cafeteria and the lobby, waiting for the bell to ring, so the hallways were pretty empty.

As I passed by classrooms, I could see some of the students through the tall rectangular windows on the doors. At this time of day, the rooms were filled with seventh and eighth graders.

I turned the corner and started down another hallway. The sunlight was hitting the ground just right, glaring off the polished floor and hitting me right in the eyes. The first floor was covered in carpet, but the second floor was 100% linoleum.

The hallway I was walking down was still in the 600's.

Brody wanted me to find him in room 801, which meant I still had two corridors to get through.

I knew I'd be fine as long as there weren't hall monitors roaming the hallways. Or even worse, any of the red—

I heard a swooshing sound come from behind me. I spun in place, but didn't see anything. There was nothing. It was completely silent, and the air was calm.

But to me, it felt a little *too* calm.

Another swoosh came from the opposite direction. I spun again, but saw nothing.

"Great," I whispered. And then I spoke up. "Helloooo?"

Another swoosh, again from behind, but this time when I turned around, I was facing a small herd of red ninjas. They were at the end of the hall, about ten feet away from me, but their masks were different – still red, but with a different pattern.

"Of course," I huffed, pulling my ninja mask from the

hood of my sweatshirt, and yanking it down the front of my face.

At that second, the ninjas started sprinting after me. I had to bolt. I didn't even have enough time to take my hoodie off.

I sprinted down the hallway, my feet hardly making a sound. All I wanted to do was get away from Wyatt's red ninjas, not alert the entire second floor that we were running around.

At the corner of the hallway, I dropped to my thigh and slid along the ground, popping myself back up after I cleared the bend.

COMING SOON...

THE UNTIMELY DEATH OF CHASE COOPER'S SOCIAL LIFE

NEW MASK??

YELLOW CAPE??
(TRUST ME, IT'S YELLOW)

But standing in my way was *another* red ninja. It *had* to have been Wyatt because he was simply standing in place, like he was watching his ninjas carry out his orders. Like the ninjas chasing me, Wyatt was wearing a different style mask, but he also wore a yellow cape that draped over his left shoulder. He must've upgraded his armor.

Suddenly, two hands grabbed at my forearms from behind, while a third hand clutched the part of my ninja mask on top of my head.

The second I felt the cloth slide up on my face, I pulled my arms free from the two ninjas that were holding them. Then I grabbed my mask and pulled it back down before it had been completely ripped off.

Wyatt was still standing several feet away. He wasn't doing anything except staring at the scuffle with his arms crossed.

The only thing I could ever trust about Wyatt was the fact that he refused to unmask me in front of anyone. Sure, a few kids know who I am, but most didn't, and for some reason, *that* was the only area Wyatt chose to respect.

So why were things different in that hallway? Why was he just standing there as his ninjas tried to take my mask off?

Again, I felt fingers slide on the back of my mask. Those kids were determined to unmask me!

I dropped to the ground and rolled backward, away from the three ninjas that were tripping over each other to get their hands on my mask.

Room 801 was only one hallway down. All I had to do was get there without being unmasked, so I started running as fast as I could, not even caring that my feet stomped on the tiles like a jackhammer.

As I passed Wyatt, he stared daggers at me the entire time, but he never tried to stop me. Something was off about him though – his eyes – they looked... *different.*

Once I got to the end of the hall, I tried to drop into another controlled slide, but the floor was too slick, and I dropped like a ragdoll instead.

I rolled wildly past the turn with my arms and legs flopping around as if all my muscles had magically disappeared from my body.

Thankfully, a set of metal lockers built into bricks tenderly stopped me, which is another way to say that I slammed into the wall.

"*Nailed it*," I groaned, rolling to my knees.

The sound of a door opening nearby shocked me back to reality, and I quickly sat up, pulling my mask off my face and stuffing it into the back of my hood.

Dizzy, and confused, I forced an awkward smile, trying my best to hide the fact that I just gotten my butt kicked by a bunch of metal lockers.

"Chase?" a boy asked from the door that had opened.

It was Brody Valentine.

"Dude," he said. "Is that you makin' all that noise out here?"

I nodded as I painfully brought myself to my feet, grunting like an old man. I sounded like my grandpa when the doorbell rang and he was the only one around to answer it.

"Are you trying out for gymnastics or something?" he quipped.

I nodded again, trying to be funny.

Brody left the doorway and swiftly walked to the end of the hall, to where the red ninjas had just chased me.

"Brody, wait!" I said, clutching a painful cramp in my side.

73

He leaned over and peeked down the hallway, but didn't act as if anything was wrong. "What?" he asked.

I stared at him. "Oh," I said. "Is there anyone there?"

"Nope," Brody said, shaking his head. "Was there supposed to be?"

"Uhhhhh, no," I replied. "I mean, like, why are you looking down there?"

"I'm just making sure none of the teachers heard you banging around like a monkey with a new drum set," Brody said. He pointed at the room with the open door. "After you."

I wasn't sure where the red ninjas had hidden themselves. Being a ninja myself, I knew they had to be in one of the empty classrooms nearby... or behind the ceiling tiles above us... or even squeezed into some lockers. They were watching us, and it made me uneasy, but I had to let it slide. I was with Brody now, and there was a case to be solved.

I took a deep breath, and stepped room 801.

Tuesday. 12:00 PM. Room 801.

The room was dark. The only light came from television monitors mounted to the wall in front of a keyboard and mouse.

It took a second for my eyes to adjust, but when they did, I saw that Brody and I weren't alone. There were three other students sitting at a round table at the back of the room.

I lifted my hand and waved. "S'up," I said.

Brody let the door shut behind him as he walked in. Taking a seat on a small stool with wheels on it, he rolled over to the screens on the wall and tapped at the keyboard.

"Sooooo," he said softly. "Whuddup?"

"Y'know," I said. "Same stuff, different day."

"Same stuff?" Brody asked. "What's that mean? You deal with headless statues everyday? Like, is that your job?"

The kids at the back of the room laughed.

"Don't look at them," Brody said. "You're not allowed to look at them."

I wasn't sure if he was joking, so I just stared at the floor.

Brody laughed. "Dude, I'm *messing* with you!"

Good. He *was* only joking.

75

Brody clicked a button on the mouse, lighting up all the monitors at the same time. The bright screens lit up the dark area, and I was able to see the faces of the three students at the table.

Two of the kids I knew from different classes – Linus and Maddie. The third girl was someone I'd never seen before. She looked Asian, but not full Asian, like maybe she was only half.

Maddie was a good friend of Zoe's. I saw the two of them joking around in the hallways a lot. Maddie was even in the same English class as me.

I knew Linus from science. He had a seat way in the back, and actually was only in class half the time. I had no idea where he was the other half of the time.

And the third girl was the one who looked like she had a little Asian in her. She was wearing super trendy clothing, thick-rimmed glasses, and a set of huge headphones over her ears. I could hear upbeat techno music coming from the headphones.

"Hi," the Asian girl said as she pulled her headphones off her head. The music filled the room, which totally meant the volume was cranked. "I'm K-pop."

"Gidget's friend!" I said, pointing at the girl. "You like Korean pop music, which I just realized is what's playing on your headphones right now."

K-pop smirked, shrugging her shoulders. "It's like you've known me all your life," she joked.

I wasn't sure how much Gidget told K-pop. I doubted that Gidget would've said anything about the ninja clan, but I dunno. I've been wrong before.

K-pop's face stretched out a smile. "Soooo," she said. "How's Faith?"

Uhg… Gidget must've told her more than I thought. I've had a crush on Faith since the first day of school, but it wasn't like it was a secret. We weren't going out or anything, but I wasn't sure if it was because I was too much of a lamewad to officially ask her or if it was because of some other… *better* reason?

"She's good," I said, looking around the room, trying my best not to make eye contact.

"Who's Faith?" Brody asked, pretending he was clueless. It was painfully obvious that he knew exactly who

Faith was.

"Seriously?" I asked. "Do you guys all know?"

"The whole school knows, dude," Brody said. "Who cares though? So you like a girl. Whatever, right?"

I smiled. "Right."

K-pop started making smooching sounds in the back.

Even though the room was dim, I'm pretty sure everyone could tell I was blushing.

"I'm just playin' with ya," K-pop said.

"Don't mind her," Linus said. "She likes to make people uncomfortable when she first meets them. It's kind of a thing she does."

K-pop smiled. "Sorry. You can stop being all sweaty and stuff now."

I felt my forehead with my fingers. She was right. I was so embarrassed and uncomfortable that I was beginning to sweat.

Brody laughed. "Seriously," he said. "Don't worry about K-pop. She really *is* just messing with you." He turned to the Asian girl. "K-pop, leave him alone!"

Maddie slapped K-pop's arm with the back of her hand. "Yeah, leave the boy alone!"

I took a breath, wiping off the rest of my forehead sweat with the sleeve of my hoodie. There wasn't much, but enough that my skin probably glistened for a few minutes.

"Are we allowed to be in here?" I asked Brody as I glanced at the computer screens. "I mean, this doesn't seem like a place where sixth graders are allowed to be."

Brody smirked, shooting a look back to his friends. "I think we'll be fine."

I turned to the kids in the back. "I just don't wanna get detention because of this. Seems like the kind of thing where you get in so much trouble that anyone within ten feet of you also gets detention."

"It's not like that," Linus said. "I promise that it's okay. You won't get in trouble for being back here. We're all allowed. You can even say that we sort of 'own' this room."

I nodded. "Whatever you say. I'll just trust you guys."

"Good," Linus said bluntly, but with a smile.

"Chase, are you a vegan?" K-pop blurted out.

"K-pop!" Maddie said, laughing out loud. "Manners!"

K-pop giggled, and than slapped the table. "Sorry! It's just so easy when you first meet someone! You seem like you're a cool kid. That's the only reason why I keep harping on ya."

That time, I laughed too. K-pop wasn't shy around new people at all, which was awesome. I wished I could be like that when meeting someone new. And even though she was giving me a hard time, I could tell it was in good fun.

When most people give others a hard time, it's kind of hard to tell if they're being mean or not. But it wasn't like that with K-pop. I think people would say it was "charming," because even though she made me sweat, she never made me feel like I was out of place.

K-pop giggled again, and then got a serious look on her face. "So, Chase, answer the question. Vegan or not?"

I paused. "Um," I said, not sure what she wanted to hear. "I guess I don't know exactly what a vegan is…"

Everyone in the room stared at me in silence. And then at the same time, they all laughed. So did I. My group of friends would definitely have a good time with Brody and his group of friends.

Brody spun around in his chair. "So Gidget only told K-pop a little bit about the problem," he said, sighing. I think he was trying to act cool. "Why don't you tell me the *sitch*."

I made a face. "Sitch?"

Brody looked down, embarrassed. "Situation. Sorry."

I chuckled. "No, it's cool," I said pointing at the monitors. "Why don't you tell me about all this first. I didn't know we had cameras in the school."

Brody said nothing for a second, looking at his friends like he wasn't sure what to say. "Not a lot of people know about these," he explained. "Obviously the staff know, but only a handful of kids know."

"What? Only a handful of kids?" I asked, and then joked, "Like a bunch of secret agent kids or something?"

Brody let out a small laugh, but the guys in the back didn't. They sat perfectly still, watching me. I felt kind of sheepish for making a dumb joke.

"The *sitch!*" I said, changing the subject quickly. "So, you guys probably already know, but the head of James Buchanan was stolen yesterday."

"It was?" Linus asked from the table.

"Yeah," I said. "How have you *not* heard? It's what's trending in the halls this week."

Brody answered for Linus. "We've got about a million other things distracting us. Why do you care about who stole the dumb head?"

"I heard about it," K-pop said. "I guess Principal Davis is keeping the pieces in a box under his desk too. Kinda creepy, but whatever."

I let out a sigh. "My friend is taking the heat for it, but he didn't do it. He's rotting away in detention right now because someone stashed it in his book bag."

"Got it," Brody said.

"Gidget asked if you guys could see if the video cameras caught anything," K-pop added. "Brody, just play the video feed."

"Right," Brody said, tapping away at the keyboard in front of him.

79

The monitors all flashed as he punched in a code and moved the mouse around. Finally, he brought up the folder of videos from the day before.

After opening one of the folders at the top, he clicked on a video file that was from the lobby of the school.

"What time did it happen?" Brody asked.

"Right after school started," I said. "Like, within the first twenty minutes of homeroom."

"Here we go," Brody said as he clicked play on one of the files.

The screens all showed the same video of an empty lobby. Nothing was happening.

Brody grew impatient, and clicked the fast forward button on the screen. Through squiggly lines, we all watched, waiting for someone to show up in the video.

Finally, after a few minutes of fast forwarding, a figure appeared, walking through the lobby. Brody released the mouse, and the video played at normal speed.

"There," Brody said.

I leaned closer to the screen. The smell of static from all the electronics in front of me filled my nose as I kept my eyes peeled at the boy in the video.

The kid on the screen was pushing a cart in front of him that was covered with a white sheet. He was moving carefully through the lobby, bobbing his body back and forth, making sure nobody else was coming before moving a foot forward and repeating the motion.

"What's on the cart?" Maddie's voice asked.

"I don't know," I said. "I can't tell. It looks big though."

"Can you see his face?" Linus said.

"No," Brody answered. "The camera angle is too high up, and he's keeping his face down whenever he looks behind him."

And then the boy in the video pushed the cart hard, accidentally making it swerve to the left, crashing into the statue of Buchanan. As soon as he did it, the base of the statue jerked, and then bounced back and then forward again. That's when the head of Buchanan broke off from the statue's neck, smashing to the floor and cracking into three pieces.

"Boom," Brody said. "That's your guy."

The boy in the video was clearly freaking out, spinning circles and hoping that no one heard him. Even though there wasn't any sound in the video, I'm sure the head crashed pretty loudly.

And then I watched as the boy scooped up the three pieces of the statue. Again, he looked back and forth, but stopped to stare down the hall. Someone must've been coming because he immediately ran to the side of the lobby with the pieces of the statue cradled in his arms.

"When do you put it in Brayden's book bag?" I whispered to myself, watching the panicked student in the video.

What happened next confused me even more.

The boy who broke the statue, ran to the garbage bin next to the nook – the same one I had thrown the paper airplane away in.

Then he *dumped* the pieces of the statue *into* the garbage.

"Wait," I said. "He didn't keep the pieces of the statue? He just tossed them? What about Brayden? How'd they end up in his book bag?"

At the end of my question, the video feed cut out, playing a bunch of static on the screen.

"What happened?" I asked, feeling frantic. "Where'd the video go?"

Maddie, Linus, and K-pop were shuffling around in the back, just as surprised as I was that the screen went blank.

"I don't know," Brody said, clicking the rewind button. The video scrolled back, but then cut off at the same spot. "The video just stops there."

K-pop stood next to me, behind Brody's chair. "Someone deleted that part of the video," she whispered eagerly, like it was thrilling for her.

"That's not suspicious," Maddie said sarcastically. "Like, *at all*."

"Rewind it again," Linus commanded Brody.

Brody rewound the video until Linus told him to stop. Then he paused it.

Linus pointed at the boy on the screen. "We can't tell you *who* it is, but look at his arms."

I squinted, studying the arms of the boy onscreen. He was wearing a long-sleeved shirt, but the cuffs were pulled up to his elbows. There was a bunch of stuff on his forearms, but I couldn't make out what it was.

"Tattoos," Linus said. "Whoever you're looking for has tats all over his arms."

"Are you kidding me?" I said. "The dude in the video is *obviously* a kid! There's no way any sixth grader has arms loaded with tattoos!"

Linus rolled his eyes. "That doesn't mean they weren't drawn on with a pen or something."

I stared at Linus. "Ohhhhhhh," I said. "That's right."

"Just find a dude with drawings all over his arms," K-pop said. "And you'll have your guy."

"Unless he washed the drawings off," I said. "But that doesn't even get me my guy. That just gets me the guy who broke the statue… not the one who put it in my buddy's book bag."

The bell rang in the hallway. The sound of students quickly filled the quiet air.

"At least it's a place to start," Brody said, clicking the mouse again.

The picture on the screen switched to a camera from the cafeteria that was currently taking place. Something strange was happening near the stage, but it was difficult to see because the camera was too far away.

Linus noticed it too. "Zoom in," he told Brody.

Brody slid his finger up on the mouse, giving us a close-up shot of the commotion in the lunchroom. After a moment, the camera focused.

A crowd of students were gathered around a spot, shouting and pointing fingers at someone. Brody zoomed the camera in a little more, and the boy at the center of the crowd filled the screen.

It was Slug.

Two hall monitors were leading him out as Principal Davis followed with another piece of the broken statue. Slug was getting taken away for having a piece of the statue on him! It was the same thing that happened to Brayden the day before!

I didn't waste a second of time, bursting from the room that Brody and his friends were in. There was barely any time before the next class started, and I needed to get to the lunchroom before that because I had to figure out what had just happened.

Tuesday. 12:10 PM. The lobby.

I ran down the stairs to the first floor of the school, skipping two steps at a time. When I rounded the corner, I saw the broken statue of James Buchanan in the lobby. Gidget was standing in front of him with her arms crossed and a look on her face that said, "Don't mess with me."

"Gidget!" I said, slowing to a stop.

She didn't say anything. She was scowling at the door to the front office. Her twin brother must've just been taken into the principal's office.

"What happened?" I asked, waving my hand in front of her face.

"Where were you?" Gidget asked, annoyed.

"I was upstairs talking to Brody!" I said. "*You're* the one who set up that meeting!"

Gidget's angry face softened. "Oh yeah," she said. "Well, now Brayden *and* Slug have been busted with pieces of the statue."

"How?" I asked.

Gidget shrugged her shoulders. "I dunno," she said. "We were finishing up lunch when Slug opened his backpack so he could save half his cheeseburger for later when—"

"Wait," I said. "Slug was going to save half his cheeseburger for later? Like, if he's hungry in class or something?"

Gidget nodded.

"That is the most…" I said, taking a deep breath slowly. "…*awesome* idea in the universe!"

Gidget cringed. "Ugh… such *boys*," she stated. "But when he opened he bag, a piece of the statue fell out right in front of everyone."

"It must've been heavy!" I said. "How did he not know it was in there?"

"I don't know," Gidget said. "Someone had to have snuck it in when we weren't looking."

"That's so coconuts," I said. "You gotta be real sneaky to pull that off."

"Slug will be in detention for sure," Gidget said. "Does that mean Brayden's free?"

"Doubt it," I said. "Because they both had *pieces* of the statue. They both could've been in on it."

"What'd you find out with Brody?" Gidget asked.

"Not a lot," I said. "The video showed someone with a bunch of drawings on their arms, but after that, the video cut off."

"It cut off," Gidget repeated.

"Yeah," I said. "Like someone got in and deleted the rest of the footage."

"Nice," Gidget said with more than an ounce of sarcasm. "Looks like we got a good ol' fashioned mystery on our hands."

"That's not even the worst part," I said. "The kid who broke the statue threw the pieces of the head away in the trash. That means he's not even the one who framed Brayden and Slug!"

"Victor?" Gidget asked.

"Maybe," I said. "But I don't even wanna go there before we know for sure if he's the one behind it. The kid gives me the heebie jeebies."

"Alright, boss," Gidget sighed. "Looks like we're after a kid with drawings on his arms."

I nodded. "Looks like."

Wednesday. 7:30 AM. Outside the school.

The next morning, I was leaving the storage garage that was behind the school. The gym teacher was out on the field, working with the football team on some drills so it wasn't like I was alone or anything.

The entryway that I was building for the Buchanan Bash on Friday was completely done. I felt this sense of pride because it was one of the first things I'd ever finished that wasn't at the last second.

Pushing the door to the garage shut, I took a breath of ice-cold air, filling my lungs as fully as possible because I liked the way it felt. 7:30 is early for me, so anything that helps me wake up is a good thing. I'm pretty sure I was doomed to be a coffee addict when I grew up.

The grass even had a light dusting of frost – the kind you couldn't see, but could hear with every step taken. And at that moment, I could hear dozens of steps coming from behind the storage garage.

The football team was practicing in front of me, which meant it wasn't the team that was running behind the shed.

Being the careless kid I was, I decided to take a look.

I leaned against the outside wall of the garage as I slid

86

down the side, keeping an eye out for anything suspicious.

And then I saw a small pack of red ninjas, but they weren't running toward me. They were after another kid... who was *also* wearing red ninja robes.

"What in the heck?" I said.

"Cooper!" the gym teacher called out from the front of the garage.

I spun around. "Yup?"

The coach gestured toward the school. "If you're done out here, get back to the school. There's no need for you to run around the track or anything."

I looked over my shoulder to see if the red ninjas were still there, but they weren't. They had disappeared. I smiled at the coach. "On my way," I said.

Whatever I had just seen couldn't have been what I thought. It *looked* like the red ninjas were chasing after one of their own, but that couldn't be possible. They had to have been training or something, but training out in the open where they risked being seen? That was a new level of bold, even for Wyatt.

87

Wednesday. 7:35 AM. The kitchen.

Inside the school, I met up with Gidget, and we went straight for breakfast in the kitchen.

At the front of the line, I took my money from my pocket and handed it to Jesse, the cashier. He didn't even try to make an excuse for the broken register when the food rang up for free again.

The same thing happened to Gidget when she paid for her tater tots and juice.

His sleeves were still stained with black, which made my stomach turn just a little as I thought about how grimy money had to be to make someone's sleeves so nasty.

In the cafeteria, Gidget and I found a table near the stage.

I split open the top of my milk carton, but saw a black smear on the bottom of the waxy cardboard. "Nasty," I said. "Jesse got my milk carton all muddy with filth. I don't know if I can drink this anymore."

Gidget pouted as she inspected her drink. "Good," she said. "It's not on mine."

"Lucky," I said, setting my carton on the table.

"Slug's pretty upset about detention," she said.

88

I sighed. "So's Brayden," I said. "I mean, I *think* he is. I tried calling him last night, but he didn't answer."

Gidget chucked a tater tot into the air, and then caught it in her mouth. "They're bummed about having to wait around while we try and figure out this whole thing, but I think they're just mad about being so bored in detention."

"I've been there," I said. "Every minute feels like an hour."

Gidget slowly chewed on her tater tot. She looked like she wanted to say something, but had trouble finding the words. Finally, she spoke. "Slug said he's thinking about trying out for the football team."

"That's cool," I said.

"That would mean he'd be done with the ninja clan," Gidget said.

I paused. "I mean, if *that's* what he wants to do."

Gidget took a moment, catching another tot in her mouth. "If he does that, then I'm not sure I'll stick around either."

I was going to say something, but Gidget spoke over me so she could explain.

"It's not that your ninja clan is lame or anything," Gidget said. "It's just that there's not much going on in it. It's kind of..." she stopped, carefully thinking of how to put it. "Boring?"

"Boring?" I repeated, but with hardly a sound coming from my lips.

Gidget's eyes softened. "You're a great leader," she said. "Really, you are, but this whole thing just isn't what we thought it'd be."

I was without words. Was I losing my ninja clan again?

"It's not you," Gidget added. "It's me... it's us."

"Geez, Gidget," I said. "It sounds like you're breaking up with me."

"Not with you," she said. "Just with the ninja clan."

"At least I've still got Brayden," I sighed. "Just the two of us."

"Yeaaaaaaaah," Gidget said, stretching out the word. "About that – I think Slug mentioned that Brayden was gonna try out for the team too."

"Are you serious?" I asked. "But... I mean, he never said anything to me about it!"

89

Gidget stared at her milk carton.

I couldn't believe what I was hearing. The remaining members of my ninja clan, *including* Brayden, the most faithful member, were all thinking of moving on with their lives.

And it wasn't like I could stop them. I didn't want to beg for them to stay if they really didn't want to. That's not how I wanted to be. If they wanted out, then I had to respect that.

But I couldn't help but feel like this time was different. It was almost more of a bummer for them to leave because they were bored than for them to leave because they were angry.

I hated feeling like a bad leader. I thought I had moved beyond that, but there it was, staring me in the face. Maybe I just wasn't cut out to have my own ninja clan. It's like the universe had been trying to rip it away from me since the moment I got it! Maybe it was time for me to hang up my ninja robes for good this time...

Victor's face flashed in my mind, and then his words floated in my head like they were on a banner that was being pulled by an airplane he was piloting. "...*your ninjas will understand that there's really no point to your clan. That there's no point to your leadership, and that you guys just have no purpose.*"

It was a really long banner.

Scooping up my tray, I headed for the trashcans at the side of the cafeteria. Gidget must've felt bad about what she said because she immediately jumped up and followed me with her tray too. She was so distracted that she left her book bag on the floor.

"Chase, wait!" she said. "Where are you going? Would you get back here and talk to me?"

I didn't say anything as I marched toward the trashcans. I wasn't sure where I was going, but I knew I needed to get out of that cafeteria.

I heard Gidget groan. She stopped in the middle of the lunchroom, and headed back toward her book bag by the table.

About a second later, I heard a giant "*KLUNK*" sound that echoed off the walls of the cafeteria.

That was when I heard another gasp from all the students around me, along with a bunch of shocked grunts.

Stopping in the middle of the room, I turned around to

see what all the fuss was about.

Gidget was back at the lunch table, standing perfectly still, with her open book bag in her hands. She was staring at the giant stone object that landed on the table in front of her.

It was another piece of broken statue.

My fingers squeezed my lunch tray. I wanted to run to her and help, but everyone in the cafeteria had already seen what happened. If the broken piece of statue didn't crash onto the table, then maybe nobody would've noticed, but it did, and now Gidget was the center of attention.

She looked around the room as students shouted at her. Some of the kids were already yelling for any nearby teachers.

Her eyes met mine, and I didn't know what to do. What was I *supposed* to do? Help her get away? Stuff the broken statue back into her book bag? Create a distraction? It was too late for *any* of those things.

Two hall monitors wearing suits took her aside, asking her questions. She kept shrugging her shoulders and shaking her head, pointing at her book bag. I knew she wasn't getting anywhere with them because she looked so frustrated as she defended herself.

Then Principal Davis showed up, taking the piece of statue and walking Gidget out of the lunchroom.

During all that, I was still standing in the aisle, holding my lunch tray, and staring like some kind of goon. Gidget looked to me for help more than a couple times when the monitors were questioning her, but all I could do was watch.

"*Why didn't you do something?*" my brain screamed at me.

My knees shook as the hall monitors took Gidget through the lobby, toward the front offices. She wasn't gone yet, which meant I still had time. I could at least get out there to try and say *something*. *Anything* was better than nothing!

I jogged to the kitchen window with my tray in my hands. Without slowing down, I flipped my tray across the metal counter toward Jesse. Since I didn't finish my chocolate milk, the carton bounced right in front of Jesse, splashing milk all over him.

"Dude!" he shrieked.

"Sorry!" I yelled as I turned my jog into an all out sprint for the front doors of the cafeteria.

Through the tinted glass walls of the lunchroom, I could see Gidget walking into the front offices.

"Wait!" I barked as I burst through the cafeteria exit and into the lobby.

But I was too late. The last thing I saw was Gidget's face as she turned to look at me one more time before the doors to the front office clicked shut.

"Crumb," I said.

Wednesday. 11:30 AM. Lunch.

The rest of the morning went on pretty much as you'd expect at that point. Brayden, Slug, and Gidget were serving out sentences in detention. Zoe and Faith were so distracted by planning for the Bash that we hardly spoke.

I was going through the day on autopilot, racking my brain, trying to figure out who was behind the broken statue. With everything that was happening, the only thing I could do was focus on the boy with fake tattoos and hope that everything would go back to normal once I found him.

If Zoe could see me now, she'd wonder why I didn't go to the principal yet. That answer was easy – if I went to Principal Davis, I'd have to admit to having a secret ninja clan, and that wasn't something I was ready for... at least not yet anyway.

Out in the lobby, I sat on one of the benches near the nook. After everything that happened, I wasn't really in the mood to eat anything. Besides, stress always made me feel queasy.

Since it was the beginning of lunch, everyone was still in the cafeteria, leaving me with the entire lobby to myself.

The statue of James Buchanan still stood proudly, but

without a head. In the past, I'd had weird dreams where the president would visit me and help me figure out what was going on.

"I could really use some help now, James," I said. "I mean, Mr. Buchanan…er… Mr. President."

I held my breath, listening carefully for him to respond. I probably looked like a crazy person.

Then I heard the sound of someone breathing. Not close, but not too far away – like maybe it was somewhere in my head.

Was James Buchanan trying to speak to me?

I sharpened my focus, listening as the quick breaths turned into footsteps scraping against the carpet.

Good. It wasn't actually the president trying to contact me from the afterlife, which meant I *wasn't* going crazy.

The footsteps grew louder until they sounded like they were right down the hallway next to the lobby.

I glanced over and saw Wyatt running at full speed, grunting loudly as he turned the corner, disappearing again.

After that, two red ninjas appeared and disappeared the same way Wyatt had. What the heck were they running from?

And then it hit me… Wyatt wasn't running *with* his

ninja clan – he was running *away* from them. They were chasing after him… but *why?*

"That does it," I said. The case of the broken statue had wound me up like a tangled ball of string, and following the red ninjas sounded like the perfect distraction.

I snuck down the side of the lobby so I was out of sight from anyone in the cafeteria. A few feet into the hallway, I pulled my ninja mask out of my hood and slipped it down the front of my face.

I leaned over, checking the area for Wyatt and his red ninjas. Why were they chasing after him? Were they playing some kind of weird game of ninja tag or something?

At the very end of the hallway, I saw the red ninjas leaning against the lockers, catching their breath and saying something to each other. They kept pointing back and forth between two different directions that Wyatt could've gotten away in.

Suddenly, one of the empty classroom doors next to the ninjas burst open, and Wyatt jumped out, sprinting away from the two ninjas, and back toward me.

"Uh-oh," I said, pressing my body against the wall, hoping that Wyatt would just run past me.

"S'up, man?" came a gruff voice from my right.

I jumped back, frightened from the kid who magically appeared. And then I jumped back again when I saw that it was another red ninja who had talked to me. And he was *big*.

The red ninja reached for the top of my mask, the same way the other red ninjas tried before.

I arched backward, barely dodging the boy's hand, but then bumped into Wyatt at the same time he was passing by.

Wyatt grabbed the back of my hoodie and pulled me away from the big red ninja. Spinning in place in the hall, I caught my footing, and bounced into a sprint right next to him.

"*What* are you doing?" Wyatt squawked angrily as we ran together.

"What are *you* doing?" I asked, my voice muffled through my ninja mask.

"It's not your business!" Wyatt said. "Why are you even out here? Why aren't you eating lunch?"

"That's not *your* business!" I said.

It was a pretty childish argument to have while running away from some ninjas.

At the end of the hallway, Wyatt took a hard left turn. I was going so fast that I had to throw my foot against one of the lockers to keep myself from crashing into it. For about half a second, it was like I was one of those ninjas that could run on the sides of buildings. It was pretty sweet.

The red ninjas turned the corner right behind us and continued their chase.

"What is this? What's happening?" I shouted. "I feel like I've completely gone insane!"

Wyatt turned down another hall. He grabbed my hoodie again just as I was about to run past him, and then he pulled me into another classroom.

We pressed our backs against the wall, staying out of sight as the ninjas in the hallway bolted past the door.

The red ninjas couldn't have been that smart. How could they lose the kids they were chasing and *not* check inside one of random open classrooms in the hall?

Probably because the classroom was full of students.

My heart dropped when I realized I was standing in front of an entire room full of kids, all staring at me like I was some kind of nutcase wearing a ninja mask.

The teacher was at the front of the class. He had been in

the middle of writing math problems on the whiteboard, but at that moment, he was just as surprised as the rest of the people in that room.

"Whoops," I mumbled.

I heard Wyatt chuckle.

"Can I help you two?" the teacher asked, confused.

In front of all the wide-eyed students, I moved in slow motion back to the door. Like, maybe if I moved slowly enough, they wouldn't see me. But it didn't work. It just made things worse. It was the most awkward thirty seconds of exiting a room I'd ever been a part of. Trust me, I've exited rooms *thousands* of times. It was just embarrassing.

Once I was back in the hallway, I heard Wyatt shut the classroom door behind us.

He glared at me for a moment, and then started walking back toward the lobby.

"Wait!" I said, pulling my mask off my face. "What the *junk* was that all about?"

Wyatt stopped, putting his hands on his hips. He sighed deeply. "Like I said, it's not your business."

"Did you just *save* me back there?" I asked. "Did you just pull me aside so your red ninjas wouldn't get me?"

Wyatt huffed, but didn't answer. It was obvious he was hiding something.

"Awwww," I sang sarcastically. "Even though you hate me, you still care enough to protect me. How sweet."

"Knock it off," Wyatt sneered.

"Then tell me what's up!" I demanded.

Wyatt paused. His jaw muscles created small waves in his cheeks as he grit his teeth. Finally, he spoke. "I'm having some… *trouble* with my ninja clan, alright?"

"Oh?" I said, feeling a sense of delight somewhere deep in my body, around my stomach I think.

Wyatt snarled, clearly upset. "I *might* have made a mistake by trying to make a ninja clan the size of a small army. And now my ninjas *might* be a little bit out of control. Geez, and *after* I got everyone cool new ninja masks! The high tech ones too, with the fabric that keeps your skin cool when you sweat! It's like astronaut fabric!"

"Out of control?" I asked. "What's that mean?"

"Just don't be surprised if you see another ninja clan pop up soon," Wyatt muttered. The anger in his face disappeared, melting into a more worried expression.

"*Another* clan?" I repeated. "Are you kidding me right now?"

"I wish," Wyatt blurted. "I can honestly say I never saw this coming."

"But why were your red ninjas chasing after you?" I questioned.

Wyatt continued, but I could tell he really didn't want to talk. "The new ninja clan *might* be looking for a new leader, and the way that they become the leader would be to steal my ninja mask… or *yours*."

I gasped. "*That's* why those guys kept trying to pull my mask off! But why in the heck would you give the order to do that? Why would you tell them to steal *your* mask?"

"Maybe b'cause I didn't give the order, Chase!" Wyatt growled at me.

"But if you didn't give the order, then…" I stopped, confused. "Wait… are you still the leader of your red ninjas?"

Wyatt's face scrunched so hard that I thought a black hole had formed in the middle of his brain, and was pulling him in. He didn't answer my question. Instead, he threw his arms in the air, made a "bah!" sound, and stormed off.

I didn't follow him. I was floored. Wyatt had been working for months on his red ninja clan, building it and recruiting half the school for it. And now, was he telling me that he lost control of it? If that were true, I wasn't looking forward to meeting the kid who took it from Wyatt.

Looking over my shoulder, I checked to see if I was being followed by any red ninjas. I was relieved when I saw an empty hallway.

Buchanan School was a rough place, but from what Wyatt had said, it sounded like things were about to get much worse.

Thursday. 7:00 AM. Before school.

When I got to school the next morning, I went straight for the storage garage down by the track. I'm not one to wake up early more than a couple days in a row, but I wanted to keep checking on my project for the Bash.

The entryway I had built was finished and safe in the garage, but I had a nagging thought that either The Scavengers *or* the red ninjas would try to mess with it. I was happy when I saw that everything was still "thumbs-up."

I shut the garage door behind me and jiggled the handle, making sure it was completely closed.

"Everything cool in there?" a voice behind me said.

It was Victor.

I tried to hide the fact that he startled me when I turned to face him.

"Everything's fine," I said.

"Good," Victor replied, not actually caring about the entryway. "Sooooo…" he sang as if we were old buddies. "What's new with you?"

I stared at the leader of The Scavengers. "You know exactly what's new with me," I said. "You're going around framing my friends for breaking the statue!"

Victor looked offended. "*Whaaaaaat?* No," he said. "I would *never* do such a thing!"

"Whatever. I know it's you."

"I don't know, man," he said, shrugging his shoulders. "I mean, that's a pretty bold accusation. Do you have any proof or anything?"

Victor knew I had nothing on him, which was exactly why he was egging me on. "No," I said. "Not yet, but I will... somehow."

"Won't happen," Victor sighed. He was so confident that it was like he didn't have a care in the world.

"What do you want?" I asked impatiently.

"I just wanted to see how you were doing this week," Victor answered with a sly smile. "I know you're going through a lot, and I just thought that, y'know, maybe you'd need a friend or something."

I didn't say anything. I didn't even *want* to.

Victor burst out laughing. "I'm sorry," he said with a hand over his chest. "I can't keep a straight face anymore. No, hey, honestly, I just wanted to see what a mess you were in person, that's all."

Was this kid psychotic? Who does that? Who goes right to the person they're picking on just to see the look on their face?

Victor leaned to the side to get a better look at the storage garage door. "Whatcha got in there?"

"Nothing," I said quickly, trying to think of a good reason why I'd be in the school's garage. I didn't want to let Victor know that I had a project inside. "I was just, um... practicing some... dance moves..."

Nailed it.

"Dance moves, huh?" Victor asked. "Whatever, dude."

From the look on his face, I could tell that Victor believed I had actually spent all morning dancing. I stepped past the leader of The Scavengers, ending our conversation.

As I walked toward the school, I expected Victor to shout at me, the same way Wyatt did whenever I turned my back on him, but Victor never did. He was different from Wyatt, and that terrified me.

My cellphone vibrated in my front pocket. Pulling it out, I slid my finger across the screen, unlocking it.

It said I had one unread message from Brody Valentine.

"Not sure when you'll get 2 school, but if u have time, I'm in the library. Find me. It's important."

Pushing my phone back into my pocket, I felt a chill run down my back, all the way to my toes. Hopefully Brody had some good news. I was really in need of some good news.

I turned to look back at the garage, to see if Victor was still there, but he wasn't. He was gone.

Five minutes later, I was in the library, keeping an eye out for any zombies that might've been in there.

Library zombies – kids who hung out in the library because they were allowed to use the Internet to study, but instead, used that time to text their friends, obsess over their online profiles, and watch videos of kittens that were so adorable that it turned their brains to mush.

If a library zombie caught you, you're finished for the rest of the period. One tiny glimpse at a kitten video is all it takes to suck you into the black hole of other cute videos.

Lucky for me, it was too early for library zombies. Funny enough, most of the library zombies were probably breakfast zombies in the cafeteria at that moment.

Breakfast zombies are pretty much self-explanatory.

The library was mostly empty, except for the librarian and a few other teachers sipping coffee and reading newspaper websites on their laptops. If it were fifty years ago, those teachers would be reading a *real* newspaper. Actually, if it were only *ten* years ago, they'd probably still be reading a real newspaper.

Brody was the only student in the library, sitting at a gigantic table by himself, studying a bunch of photos spread out in front of him.

"Valentine," I said in a menacing tone.

"Cooper," Brody replied. He tried spinning his chair like an evil villain, but the chair didn't spin. Instead, he just gripped the sides and leaned his body far enough that the chair bobbed back and forth until finally facing me. Instead of looking like a villain, he looked like a bobble-head.

"Whaddup?" I asked, taking a seat across from him on the other side of the table.

"Good news!" Brody said with his face lit up, but then his smile turned into a frown. "Then bad news, and I think even worse news…"

"Nice," I sighed.

Brody slid a photo across the table. "So after we found out that part of the video from the security camera had been deleted, I searched a bunch of other video feeds to see if any of *those* cameras saw anything."

I pulled the photo closer to me. It was actually a stack of photos that Brody printed. They were screenshots from another video that he must've found. The timestamp in the corner showed that each photo was about three seconds apart. The one on top was of the empty lobby, *after* the kid with the fake tattoos had broken the statue.

"Those are taken from a camera that was farther down the hall," Brody explained. "The video is zoomed in, but it's still way too far away to see the face of the kid who broke the statue, but... there's more."

I flipped through the stack of printed photos, watching as the kid with the fake tattoos picked up the pieces of the broken statue and tossed it into the garbage can.

After that, he took his cart and wheeled it away in the

opposite direction.

The timestamp said that it was about a minute later when *another* student showed up in the lobby, headed straight toward the garbage can. It was like he knew exactly what was in there.

The kid was covered in shadow, which made it hard to see his face.

"Who is that?" I asked Brody.

Brody scratched his eyebrow. "Keep going," he said softly.

I flipped each photo over, watching the screenshots play out like a glitchy movie.

The boy reached into the garbage can, bending in half so he could grab it from the bottom. Then he pulled out the three pieces, carefully pushing them so that they fit where they belonged.

After that, he stuffed the statue's head into his book bag, zipped it up, and walked down the hallway, toward the camera that was filming him.

The shadows on his face crept upward as he got closer and closer until finally, I could see exactly who it was...

It was Brayden.

Brayden was the one who took the statue from the garbage can.

"I can tell by the look on your face that you got to the page with Brayden," Brody said. "I'm sorry."

"I don't understand," I whispered.

"I don't either," Brody said. "But keep going."

Glancing up, I spoke with barely a sound coming from my mouth. "There's more?"

Brody nodded.

I kept flipping through the stack of printed photos. The camera had changed from one inside the school to one outside by the dumpsters.

"No, dude," I said, remembering the camera I had seen when I went to visit with Victor.

The printed photos continued to show me what I didn't want to see. Brayden walked out of the cafeteria doors, looking around to make sure he was alone. Then he stopped about five feet away from the dumpsters.

That's when a girl walked out to meet him. It was Naomi. She was holding her new cellphone in front of her.

Victor soon appeared farther back. Brayden then took two pieces of the statue out of his book bag, and handed them to Naomi. That was the last photo.

He handed them to Naomi!

"Victor and Naomi are two dangerous kids," Brody said. "And Brayden is right there talking to them."

"I don't know what I'm looking at," I said. "What happened?"

Brody shrugged his shoulders. "It looks like your buddy is playing along with Naomi and Victor. Did you notice that Brayden kept one of the broken pieces in his bag?"

"What do you know about Victor?" I asked.

Brody shook his head. "Nothing," he admitted. "Just that he's a bad apple. That's what Linus and Maddie told me, but they didn't tell me why. They said I need to stay away from him and from Naomi."

I nodded. "They're right," was the only thing I said. It wasn't my place to tell Brody what was going on. He helped me out enough, and the less he knew about The Scavengers, the better.

Sinking in my chair, I exhaled slowly, afraid that I was going to pass out.

Brody took the stack of photos and stuffed them into his book bag. After he apologized for having to give me such bad news, he said goodbye and headed out of the library.

I just sat there at the table, staring off into space.

I couldn't believe how everything that was important to me was flipped around that week. Victor hardly did anything at all, but I felt like he had won. I felt like The Scavengers had won. His revenge wasn't loud or explosive. It was far worse – subtle and totally destructive.

I wasn't a good leader, and he showed it to me by taking my ninjas away, one by one until I was alone. But the worst part was that he was able to get *Brayden* on his team.

And I thought if there was anyone who had my back no matter what, it was Brayden. I guess I was wrong.

There it was…the last nail in my coffin. I was done. I couldn't see any point in fighting after that. Without my friends, there just wasn't a reason. The Scavengers won, and they barely had to even try. That's how weak my whole world was. Everything I had worked to build since the beginning of school was built on a bed of marshmallows.

Thursday. 7:30 AM. The cafeteria.

I sat in the library, stewing in self-pity for a few minutes before deciding to take my little party to the cafeteria. Plus I felt awkward being all alone in the middle of the library.

The cafeteria was better, but not by much. During breakfast, it was never packed with students. It was only a bustling sea of activity during lunch.

A table near the corner of the lunchroom was open, so I claimed it. I watched as students stuffed their faces with cinnamon rolls and sausage biscuits. None of the other kids in there knew that The Scavengers existed, and I felt jealous about that. How I *wished* I could eat breakfast in blissful ignorance.

A few minutes before breakfast was over, Jesse shut the doors to the kitchen so nobody else would go through the line. Once it latched, he turned around and gave me one of the worst evil eyed stares I had ever seen. It was so wretched that I could sense it from all the way across the cafeteria.

Wonderful. Someone *else* was upset with me. What more was this week going to bring?

Jesse stomped across the room until he was standing at the end of my table. Again, his sleeves were stained with black grime. Punching his angry fists down, he scolded me. "You soaked me with chocolate milk yesterday!"

I shook my head, baffled. "What are you talking about? No, I didn't!"

"Yes, you did!" Jesse said. "Right before you ran out of the cafeteria, you threw your tray at me!"

"Oh, right," I said, remembering that I wanted to get to Gidget before she went into the principal's office. That's why I threw the tray. "Sorry, dude, it was an accident."

But Jesse wasn't listening. "I can't believe you just wasted that whole carton of chocolate milk! You hardly took a sip! Get a drink of water from the fountain if all you want is a gulp of liquid!"

Something in me snapped. Not like an angry snap, but like a "please-stop-talking-to-me" snap.

I must've been more upset than I thought because I raised my voice louder than I meant to. "I didn't drink it because you left some grimy money dirt all over the bottom of my drink!" I said loudly, in front of the whole cafeteria. "Look at your sleeves, dude! They're caked with dirt! At least pull them up when you're working the register!"

Jesse looked at me like I was a crazy fool. And then he pulled both sleeves up on his forearms, realizing what I was upset about. "Sorry, man," he said, changing his tone instantly. "These smears aren't from dirty money. They're just from the marker I use to draw on my arms. Sometimes I get bored and doodle on myself. My mom *hates* it because all my clothes are gross with ink."

I stared at Jesse's forearms. He had drawn all over every inch of them. Little doodles of smiley face, stars, and random skulls were sprawled across the canvas of his skin.

I sat there silently as the whole cafeteria looked at Jesse and me. The other kids in the lunchroom were staring because it sounded like Jesse and I had gotten into a yelling match.

Even Principal Davis was walking toward us, probably because he heard me shouting and wanted to make sure there wasn't any trouble.

Jesse stood at the foot of my table, trying to apologize for the marker smudge on the bottom of my milk.

And I was frozen because I knew I had just caught the kid who broke the head off the statue that was in the lobby. He was the mystery student with the fake tats on his arms.

"Uhhhh," Jesse said. "Hello?"

"*You* broke the head off the statue," I said, my voice shaking.

Jesse's face flushed with white. He let out a laugh. "What?" he said, and then repeated it. "*What?*"

I said it louder. "*You* broke the head off the statue!"

Jesse was clearly guilty because every time he tried to say something, he coughed out a laugh. "That's crazy! You're crazy!"

"I saw you in the video!" I said. "You bumped into it with your cart, making the head fall off! And then you dumped it in the trash! What was under the sheet? What were you pushing around on your cart?"

Jesse kept laughing, but his face didn't look happy. He was uncomfortable.

"What's this all about?" Principal Davis asked, standing next to the table.

I looked at Jesse, who was sweating like crazy. And then I looked at Principal Davis who was only trying to keep things quiet in the lunchroom.

With wide-eyes, Jesse looked at me, and then to Principal Davis, and then back to me.

Nobody said a word.

Finally, Jesse spun around, sprinting away, but it wasn't far. The cafeteria table behind him did a pretty good job of stopping him in his tracks.

Jesse dropped to the ground, moaning in pain as he held his arms around his stomach.

"Son, are you alright?" Principal Davis asked as he helped Jesse to his feet.

Jesse's eye caught mine again. I pressed my lips together and shook my head at the boy.

The guilt must have been too much for him. "Fine!" he roared. "I did it, alright? I broke the head off the statue! It was me, okay? You happy now?"

Principal Davis furrowed his brow, shocked.

I just kept my butt in my seat, surprised that Jesse was confessing. Maybe he was a lot like me, and his guilt had been eating away at him all week. He was like a balloon that was ready to burst.

"But it was an accident!" Jesse said. "I swear! I didn't mean to break the statue!"

Principal Davis was staring straight ahead, trying to make sense of the situation. "*What* are you talking about?"

"The head of the statue!" Jesse said. "I broke it off when I bumped into it wheeling that stupid printer around!"

Suddenly, the voice of a woman screeched from across the room. It was the janitor, Miss Chen-Jung. "My printer! You stole the printer from the maintenance closet! You little thief!" she howled as she ran across the cafeteria.

Principal Davis put his hand up to calm the janitor down. "Slow it down, Miss Chen-Jung," he said. "Give him some room to talk."

Jesse paused, sitting on top of the next table. Everyone in the cafeteria was silent, listening as he spoke. "I nailed the statue with the printer."

"You *stole* it!" Miss Chen-Jung said harshly.

"I borrowed it!" Jesse said defensively.

"But why?" I asked.

"To print free lunch vouchers," Jesse admitted.

Principal Davis scratched his head. "Why would you print those?"

"Because the registers have been broken all week," I said, speaking for Jesse.

"No," Jesse said, and then paused. "I just said that to keep people from asking too many questions. I've been... I've been ringing everyone's lunch up as free, and then pocketing the money. I used the printer to print those free lunch vouchers so I wouldn't get caught."

The principal shook his head.

I was perplexed because it was weird that Jesse would just fess up the way he did. Most kids try to make excuses and lie about doing things like that.

Jesse covered his face. "I couldn't do it anymore," he said. "I only wanted to get around eighty bucks for a new skateboard deck! Honestly, eighty bucks and that was it! But I never counted the money until about halfway through the week! I thought, y'know, small bills would take awhile to get up to eighty, but after the third day, I counted up all the money, and..."

"And how much was it?" Principal Davis asked.

"It was over *six thousand dollars!*" Jesse said, burying his face into the palms of his hands.

Half the kids in the cafeteria sat up, shocked.

Jesse went on. "I felt *terrible* about it. Plus, those guys who are in detention because the pieces kept falling out of their backpacks! I just... I just... I'm sorry."

I couldn't say I didn't feel bad for the kid. He might've taken a ton of money from the school, but it was obvious he was torn up about it.

Even the janitor felt sorry for him. She placed her hand on his shoulder and awkwardly patted it a couple times. "There, there, human child."

Principal Davis stopped Jesse from saying anything else in front of the other students. Jesse had said enough. Anything else he wanted to say would have to wait until he was in the principal's office with his parents.

Once things settled down in the cafeteria, I took a deep breath, wondering why the heck I didn't feel any better.

I finally figured out who was behind the cracked statue, which meant that my friends would be out of detention within the hour. That should've been great news!

But that's when it all came back to me – the screenshots from the security cameras. Brayden was free from detention, but that didn't make me feel any better about the whole thing. For some reason, he was working with The Scavengers, and I knew that sooner or later, I'd have to ask him why.

Thursday. 11:30 AM. Lunch.

I wasn't surprised to see a new face behind the register in the kitchen during lunch. It was a girl whose name was Beatrice. I only knew that because of the plastic nametag pinned to her shirt. It was an old fashioned name for such a trendy young girl.

She took my dollar fifty and placed a mini cupcake on my tray. "Thank you," she said.

"Um," I said, staring at the tiny cupcake. "What's the deal with the small baked item?"

"Oh," Beatrice said, smiling like a doll. "I'm part of the '*Cupcake Kids.*' We're a club for girls to learn skills and take trips and stuff. We'll be having a bake sale in a few weeks, and these cupcakes are a small sample of what we'll have there."

I stared at the cupcake on my tray. "Huh," I grunted. "I've never heard of the Cupcake Kids before."

Beatrice smiled. "We're pretty new," she said. "I'm sure you'll hear more about us pretty soon."

"Thanks for the cupcake," I said.

"No," Beatrice said. "Thank *you.*"

Before picking my tray up from the conveyor belt, I asked, "Since you're Jesse's replacement, do you know what

113

happened to him?"

"His fate is in the hands of the school now," Beatrice said sadly, but then added, "Just kidding. As long as he returns every penny he stole, he'll only get suspended for a week."

"Oh, good," I said, feeling relieved.

I was happy to hear that Jesse was gonna be alright. A week suspension is pretty bad, but it could've been *much* worse for him. Six thousand dollars isn't exactly a small amount of money. If he had *kept* it, and the school had launched an official investigation, Jesse could've been nailed with juvie.

When I stepped out of the cafeteria, I searched the room for a place to sit. After a moment, I saw an empty table right at the center of all the other kids. It wouldn't have been my first choice, but since it was my only one, I made my way down the aisle.

I held my tray higher than normal to keep it from bumping into students at other tables. Pretty sure I said "Sorry!" to more than a few kids because of that.

Brayden, Gidget, and Slug were nowhere to be seen, which was good news for me. My brain was still spinning because of the photos Brody showed me in the library. If I had to talk to Brayden right now, I'm not sure what I'd say. I'd probably just stare at him the way a baby stares at a stranger – wide-eyed and drooling.

Finally, I set my tray down on the empty table. When I sat, I could barely see the sides of the cafeteria.

At almost the same instant, a student sat on the other side of the table, across from me.

It was Naomi.

I sighed, leaning my head against my hand, jabbing at my food with my fork. I was too drained to care that Naomi had sat with me.

Naomi took her phone from her pocket, and started filming me again.

"Seriously?" I asked. "Give it a rest."

Naomi's mouth tightened into an embarrassed smile. "Sorry," she said, setting her phone on the table, but face up so I could see she had turned it off. "I'm just so pumped about this phone."

"So I've seen," I said.

"Don't take it personally," Naomi said, lifting her book

bag and setting it next to her lunch tray. Something inside made a "*CLINK*" sound. "I've been filming everything."

"Riiiight," I said. "Because you're a Scavenger, and Scavengers spy on everyone everywhere."

Naomi didn't say anything. She unzipped her bag and reached her hand in, fishing around for something.

I took the mini cupcake that Beatrice had given me, and popped the whole thing into my mouth. "Mmm," I said with cheeks full of dry cupcake. "These are *not* good. How was yours?"

"I'd love to tell you they were totes sweet, but I guess I wouldn't know," Naomi said, and then arched her neck so she was looking back at the kitchen. "*Would I, Beatrice?*"

"She forgot to give you one?" I asked.

"Right." Naomi made quotation marks with her fingers. "*Forgot.*"

"Why are you sitting with me?" I finally found the nerve

to ask.

Naomi blinked, like she was trying to think of a good way to answer. "I don't know," she said honestly. "The past couple of weeks have been tough on me."

I laughed. "Tough on *you?* What about *me?* What about everything that's happened to *me* since learning about your little club of creepy spies?"

"I know," Naomi murmured. "I guess I won't leave you alone because I want things to feel normal."

"What's normal?" I asked, setting my fork down. There was no way I was going to be able to eat at that point.

"Sitting with you during lunch," Naomi said. "Talking about *nothing*. Giving each other a hard time because of some dorky thing we did or said."

I pushed my tray to the side, and let my head drop on the table. My forehead thunked hard enough that Naomi's book bag made another "*CLINK*" sound.

Normally, I would've been a little crazy because Naomi had the nerve to sit with me during lunch. It didn't surprise me that she and Victor were the ones behind framing the kids from my ninja clan.

But it was because of Brayden that I felt so defeated. I was numb, and I didn't even care that Naomi was trying to speak to me.

I just gave in.

Naomi reached into her book bag again, and pulled out a small teacup. She set it gently next to her lunch tray and ran her fingers against the rim.

There wasn't anything special about the teacup. In fact, it looked like it had been broken at one time. All along the sides of the cup were cracks that had been filled with golden colored sparkly glue.

"Nice cup," I said. "Do you bring your own salad dressing to school too?"

Naomi didn't pick up my joke. "No," she said, pouring her juice into the teacup.

I raised my head a bit, watching her carefully pour her drink. "What is this? I've never seen you do this before."

"It's something I've only started doing about a week ago," Naomi said. "It helps remind me of who I am."

I chuckled nervously because I had no idea what she was talking about. She sipped at the teacup, keeping her pinky finger out. It was bold. Kids would make fun of her if they saw her – a sixth grader playing tea party in the middle of the lunchroom? That was social death, but the thing about Naomi was that she didn't give a rip about what others thought of her.

Every molecule in my body wanted to be angry with this girl who had betrayed me. The girl who made half the school hate me. The girl who took my ninja clan away from me. But I just couldn't, at least, not at that moment in the cafeteria.

So I gave in, and acted like she was an old friend. I have to admit, it was easier than I thought it would be.

"Naomi," I said. "I'm really struggling this week."

"I know," she said, sipping some juice from her cup. "I used to be in your ninja clan. I know how badly you deal with stress."

I couldn't help but laugh. "Some of the stress is from you though! Like, you're the one that's messing with me!"

Naomi shook her head. "It's Victor this time," she said. "Not me."

"I know that Brayden went to you with the broken pieces of the statue," I said. "I know you were there with Victor."

Naomi didn't say anything.

"You're probably the one putting those statue pieces in everyone's book bags too, huh?" I said, hoping I was wrong.

Naomi leaned forward. "It *wasn't* me putting the statue pieces in their bags," she said.

"Then who?" I asked.

Naomi shrugged her shoulders. "Could've been anyone," she said. "There are Scavengers around this whole school. They're probably even listening to us talk right now."

I rolled my tongue in my mouth, peeking out of the corner of my eye to see if anyone was staring. Nobody was.

"Why did Brayden do it?" I asked.

Again, Naomi shrugged her shoulders. "I don't know. He just showed up with the pieces from the statue. I bounced before Victor and Brayden talked."

I shook my head, sighing. "I don't know what to do anymore," I said.

"What do you mean?" Naomi asked, pouring more juice into her teacup.

"This whole year has been one huge struggle for me," I said. "It's almost like the school just wants to crush my spirit, but I've refused to give in... until now."

Naomi set her teacup down. "Why now?"

"Because," I said. "Because I was too thick-headed to see that it was a battle I wasn't winning. Wyatt, the red ninjas, The Scavengers, you... all of you have pushed against me, and for some reason I just kept pushing back."

Running her finger along the rim of her teacup, Naomi said nothing.

I don't know why, but it was like I cracked open the door to my thoughts and I couldn't get it shut again. I just kept talking. "I've worked so hard to be a good leader – even Victor knew it, which was what he was trying to take from me this week. Well, it looks like he won. He did it, and without barely lifting a finger. If I was any good at being what I wanted to be, then it shouldn't have been so easy for him to win."

"I know," Naomi said softly. She sounded really sad.

"Victor has shown me who I really am," I said. "And I know that was his point. I was already on the edge. All he needed to do was nudge me a bit more."

"Aren't we all on the edge though?" Naomi asked.

"No?" I said. "I dunno, maybe? I'm just... I'm so tired, Naomi. I'm so tired of trying to be strong *all* the time. My ninja clan has always looked to me for leadership. My friends have always counted on me to be there when something went wrong. Everyone expects me to just know what I'm doing!"

"I think everyone feels that way," Naomi said, slightly smiling.

And then I finally found exactly what I was trying to say. "I just want someone to tell me that it's okay to struggle. That I'm even *allowed* to! That it's okay to not be strong all the time!"

Naomi stared at me with eyes as big as the rings of Saturn. I was beginning to worry that maybe I had said too much, and now her brain was sizzling to a crisp.

I opened my carton of milk and took a swig. Talking that much always made my mouth dry. "Sometimes I just wish I had never started my ninja clan. Life would be a lot easier."

"I'm only going to say this once to you," Naomi said. "Because I feel kind of weird about giving 'life' advice to anyone without feeling like I am in a cheesy movie about growing up... but it *is* okay to struggle. You're allowed to. We're *all* allowed to, even though nobody ever tells us that."

I looked at my friend across the table as she continued.

"Since the beginning of the school year, your biggest fight has been with yourself," Naomi said. "You've tried to be perfect, and I have to give it you, you've done a darn good job at getting close to it."

I wasn't sure what to say. I was already starting to feel embarrassed that I had said anything at all.

Naomi leaned back in her chair. "But you know what? None of that matters, does it? Does your ninja clan really matter?"

"Yes," I said. "No? I'm not sure how you want me to answer that."

"Your ninja clan," Naomi explained. "Even though it's important to you, and will always be important, doesn't really matter in the end."

I stared at Naomi's smiling face, confused. "Huh?"

"Having a ninja clan *isn't* what makes you and your team special," Naomi said. "It's the *people* in it... your *friends*. This whole time, I haven't *missed* the *ninja clan*. I *missed* being *friends* with you."

I shrugged my shoulders. I wasn't sure why I still wanted to argue. "Still feels like I've failed."

"It's cool," Naomi said, leaning forward. Her eyes sparkled like she was just "getting it" too. "Everyone fails. You're allowed to fail, Chase. You're allowed to struggle."

She took her teacup in her hand and raised it toward me.

"No thanks," I said. "I have my own drink."

119

"No, ya dingus," Naomi said, wagging the teacup at me. "I don't want to you *drink* it. I want you to *look* at it."

I stared at the cup in her hand. "Okay? It's an old busted up teacup. So?"

"Kintsugi" she said.

"Kint-wha?" I replied.

"It's not the same cup that I used to have," Naomi said, admiring the teacup, and running her fingers along the cracks of the porcelain. "I broke this when I was, like, three-years-old. My dad glued it back together with some sparkly glue, and then explained what the term 'kintsugi' meant."

"Sounds Japanese," I said.

"It is," Naomi said. "You know that I'm a quarter Japanese, right?"

I chuckled. "Yeah," I said, lying through my teeth.

Naomi continued. "It means '*golden joinery.*' My dad said that it was the art of repairing pottery with gold lacquer, or in this case, gold colored sparkly glue."

I studied the cracks in the teacup that Naomi was holding. The sparkles caught the light, glimmering like a billion tiny diamonds.

Naomi continued. "It's the idea that this cup is more beautiful because it's been broken."

"But you could've just used white glue," I said. "And hidden the fact that the cup was ever broken at all."

"You're missing the point," Naomi said. "The sparkly gold glue makes the cracks obvious because that's what's so special about the teacup. We don't want to hide the fact that it broke... that it struggled... because that's an important part of the teacup's story." She turned the cup slowly in her hand. "No other cup... will *ever* look like *this* cup."

"That's why you've been using it this week?" I asked.

Naomi paused. "I've always kept it in my bag," she said. "I've just never used it before. I've made a lot of mistakes. Being a Scavenger was one of them. Hurting you... was another one."

I stared at the table. That was one of the heaviest conversations I'd ever had since being at Buchanan School, and I've had a couple of doozies before, trust me.

Everything that Naomi said about my ninja clan was spot on. It *was* important to me, and being a leader was *just* as important, but none of that even came close to how important my *friends* were.

Without my friends, what was the point? What was the point to all the ninja training? What was the point to figuring out insane mysteries?

I felt the warm fuzzies from the light bulb that had switched on in my head.

The whole reason I was having a pity party for myself in the first place was because Victor had won. He won by taking away my ninja clan, but it didn't matter. It wasn't like any of my friends were going to turn their backs on me because I didn't have a ninja clan anymore.

They're my friends, and I needed to be their friend.

I felt a surge of energy run through my veins. It felt good. Probably the same way a robot feels when his battery is fully charged.

My friends were more important to me than the things I wanted for myself. They were all that matter, and Victor couldn't take *that* from me.

Victor's grip, even The Scavengers grip on me... was gone.

I opened my mouth to say more to Naomi, but she had disappeared. I quickly scanned back and forth in the cafeteria, but she wasn't anywhere I could see.

The only thing left was a slip of paper on the table in front of me. I unfolded the paper and read it.

"You should probably check the principal's office for the three pieces of the statue. Davis has been keeping them in a box under his desk."

It wasn't signed, but I knew Naomi's handwriting anywhere. I couldn't tell if she was warning me, or just giving me a heads up.

The only time I could check the principal's office was early in the morning since he was always back and forth between the cafeteria and the gymnasium before school started.

All I had to do was peek into his office and check the box under his desk.

No bigs, right?

Friday. 7:10 AM. The storage garage.

The next morning, I had my dad drop me off right by the storage garage behind the school. I still hadn't spoken to Brayden, and I thought that going *through* the school risked running into him on accident.

I opened the side door to the garage and stepped inside, feeling the hot air hit my face.

The project I had worked so hard on was standing tall in the middle of the garage, surrounded by all kinds of other junk that had collected there in the past hundred years.

My project loomed over eight feet high, and was built to look like you were walking into some kind of cool robot carnival.

I hoped Zoe would dig it. The whole idea behind the Bash was to make kids feel like they were somewhere *other* than Buchanan School.

And thankfully, my project was still untouched. It would've been easy for any of The Scavengers or even the red ninjas to have found their way into the garage to destroy that which I've worked so hard to create.

I walked around the entryway, blowing dust off the various fake wires and doors that were being held in place by

122

glue. At the top of the entryway was a sign that I had created out of aluminum foil. All it said was, "Enter the Bash."

I wasn't sure who was going to wheel the entryway into the cafeteria, but Principal Davis probably had it taken care of. After all, *he* was the one who said they'd unveil it during the assembly.

After making sure everything was in order, I took a white sheet and threw it over the top of my project so that it would be hidden when it was in the lunchroom.

The football team was outside the garage, running drills and, like… *other* football practice things. Jogging back and forth with a ball maybe? That sounds about right.

The assembly was going to start at 8:00 in the morning so everyone had extra time to goof on in the cafeteria before they needed to calm down and take a seat.

Zoe had planned for *all* the students of Buchanan School to skip their homerooms so they could gather in the lunchroom. She even had a local cinnamon bun place come and set up a breakfast buffet.

Kids were going to go nuts when the assembly would start. They always did whenever my cousin was in charge of those kinds of things.

Pulling my cellphone out of my pocket to check on the time, I heard the sound of a slip of paper fall on the cold hard cement by my feet.

The piece of paper was the note that Naomi had left on the table the day before. The one that told me I should check Principal Davis's office.

Yes, I was wearing the same jeans I had on the day before… and if we're being honest then I think you should know I sometimes wore the same jeans many, *many* days in row – sometimes for weeks at a time. What? They're my *favorite* jeans, alright?

Clicking the button on top of my cellphone, I glanced at the time. There was still thirty minutes until school started, and over an hour before the assembly! Did I have time to take a peek inside the principal's office? Of course I did.

Friday. 7:25 AM. The cafeteria.

I ran back to the school, to where the cafeteria doors were. Down to the left of one those doors was another entrance that led to the area behind the stage in the lunchroom.

Once I got to the side of the cafeteria doors, I ducked my head lower than the windows so nobody eating breakfast would spot me. The windows went all the way down the side of the cafeteria. If I wanted to get to the backstage door, I had to get past the windows.

Taking my ninja mask from my hood, I slipped it over my face in the cold weather. Puffs of steam filtered through the black cloth of my mask, drifting up in front of my eyes.

Keeping crouched, I waddled like a duck, making myself lower than the windows.

Finally, when I was a safe distance from anyone in the cafeteria, I rolled to my feet and ran to the door that led backstage. Without wasting another second, I opened it and stepped through.

The warm air hit me like a bag of bricks, mostly because the air behind the stage was thick and swampy compared to anywhere else in the building. I think it had to do with all the exposed piping that ran along the walls. At least I was inside the school.

The principal's office wasn't far. The cafeteria, lobby, and front counter of the office were the only things standing in my way. It wasn't going to be easy, but nothing ever was for a ninja.

And then it struck me... why am I running around with a ninja mask? I could just walk over to the front office, and *then* slip on my mask if I needed to.

I shook my head, pulling my ninja mask off my face. "Dummy," I said to myself.

At the side of the stage, I pulled the red velvet curtain back and jumped to the floor of the lunchroom. It was still early enough that there were hardly any students in there except for Zoe and Faith, along with the crew that was going to help dish out food for the breakfast buffet.

"Chase?" Zoe asked from across the room. "Um, what're you doing on the stage? Wait, no, don't answer that. I'm sure it's got something to do with ninja stuff, and I'm not really in the mood to stress out over some crazy thing you're doing. You can tell me after all this is over."

I laughed. "You know I will."

Faith nuzzled her body into mine, holding her arm out with her cellphone. "Smile," she said, snapping a selfie with me. Then she turned and spoke. "Where the junk have you been all week?" she asked. "It's like you've been a total loner or something."

"Kind of," I said, nodding. "It's been pretty crazy... I mean, boring. A pretty *boring* week." I didn't want to bother Faith or Zoe with my problems.

Faith slugged me in the arm. "I heard you busted Jesse for breaking the head off the Buchanan statue!"

I opened my mouth for a second, and then said, "Uhhhhhh, yeah, I did. I figured that all out, but he's really the one who turned himself in."

Zoe folded her arms and spoke like a concerned parent. "That kid was really beating himself up over it," she said. "He was almost in tears when he told his side of the story to Principal Davis."

"He seemed pretty upset yesterday too," I said. "I mean, I barely said a word to him, and he broke down like an old pickup truck."

Faith and Zoe looked at me like I was a loon.

"That doesn't make any sense," Zoe said before changing the subject. "So your project – it's finished and ready to be wheeled into the school, right?"

"Of course!" I said, super proud that I had accomplished something before the deadline. "It's waiting for Principal Davis in the garage right now."

"Cool," Zoe said. "I'll let him know and he'll take care of it."

I smiled at Faith and Zoe, and then starting walking toward the exit.

"Oh, and Chase?" Zoe called out.

I turned. "Thanks."

Lifting my hand, I raised my thumb and jabbed it in the air toward her. And then, I pushed open the door and stepped into the lobby.

Friday. 7:30 AM. The lobby.

There were only fifteen minutes until school started, so students were beginning to swarm the halls of Buchanan. It's crazy how quickly the building goes from being dead silent to being stuffed with loud kids.

The front offices were just ahead of me. There were a few teachers inside the office, but not so many that I was worried about it. All I needed to do was catch a glimpse of that box Naomi mentioned to make sure that all three pieces of the statue were safely inside it.

After I walked through the doors, some adults glanced at me, but didn't say anything.

I thought about putting my ninja mask on, but it would've been pointless. I just needed to make it to the end of the hallway to where the principal's office was.

"Can I help you?" one of the office staff asked, leaning over the front counter.

I looked around, trying to figure out if the woman was talking to me.

"Yes, *you*," she said, chewing gum with one side of her mouth. "Is there something I can help you with?"

"Oh, um," I said, stumbling. "I'm just… uh…" and then

I remembered that the nurse's office was right across the hall from the principal's. I held my stomach and made my voice sound sick. "I'm not feeling too good... my tummy's um..."

The woman pressed her lips to one side, nodding like she felt sorry for me. "Someone's got soupy poopy?"

I had to bite the inside of my cheek to keep from laughing. I've never heard anyone say "soupy poopy" before in my entire life, but I knew deep in my heart, it was going to be my new favorite thing to say.

"Yup," I said, clutching my stomach. "Soupy poopy," I said with the best straight face I could muster up. "Soupy poopy... is the thing that I am struggling with this very second..."

The woman pouted. "You poor thing," she said, waving her hand down the hall. "The nurse's station is there in the back. I don't think she's in right now, but you can have a seat on the bench outside her room. She'll be back in a few minutes."

I nodded, and hobbled down the hallway, still holding onto my stomach.

As I made my way to the principal's office, I passed some of the student counselor rooms. The doors were shut so I figured I'd be safe if I put my ninja mask on.

I'm sure it was all in my head, but I always felt like I was better at stealth when I wore my ninja mask. Even if it *was* in my head, that was fine because it worked, and anything that helped me level up in stealth was okay by me.

Finally, at the end of the hall, I stood between the principal's office and the nurse's office. I checked to see if there was anyone behind me. There wasn't.

The door to Principal Davis's office was wide open, but there wasn't anyone in it. Davis was probably wandering the halls and making sure everyone was keeping in line.

His desk was near the back, in front of a giant bookshelf that had more plants on it than books. From where I was standing I couldn't see the box where Naomi had said he kept the broken pieces of the statue.

I hated that I had to go *into* the room, but I had no other choice if I wanted to check on the statue pieces. And I had to act fast since Principal Davis could return at any second.

I stayed low to the ground as I worked my way across the carpet of the office. The room had windows along the side that looked outside. The air was freezing cold because one of the windows was wide open. Who leaves a window open on freezing cold days??

The front wall of Davis's office was completely solid though – no frosted windows or open spaces for people to see me, but I had to leave his door open or else one of the school staff might've heard it slam shut.

Sliding on my knee, I turned and stopped behind the principal's desk. His leather chair was pushed all the way in, tucked under the table.

Pushed all the way into the small space where Principal Davis's legs would go was the cardboard box that Naomi had talked about. It was folded shut, but not taped.

Moving the leather chair aside, I grabbed the box and dragged it closer.

Then I pulled open the flaps, and took a look inside.

Empty.

The box was *empty*.

"Looking for something?" came a voice from the hallway.

My body freaked, making me jump up from the spot I was crouching in. Whoever was at the door was bound to see me wearing my ninja mask. It was a stupid mistake.

Lucky for me it wasn't a teacher. Unlucky for me, it was a boy wearing one of the goofy looking vulture masks. It was a Scavenger, and there was a whole bunch of his friends behind him, wearing the very same mask.

The first time I ran into The Scavengers, they were all wearing the vulture masks, but it was all a gag. They didn't actually run around wearing them all the time, but it looked as if that all changed. Maybe the idea of wearing masks had grown on them.

I'm not sure how the office staff missed a bunch of kids wearing creepy bird masks, but whatever I guess. I couldn't think about it.

"Of course," I sighed, feeling the air get sucked from my lungs.

At first I thought I was out of breath because I was scared, but then I realized it was because of the open window at the side of the room. A cold gust of wind slipped through and washed over my body.

"Where's the broken statue head?" I asked, my voice shaking a little more than I thought it would. After all this time, I guess I was still freaked out by The Scavengers.

"In a better place," the boy in the mask said with a muffled sound. "Victor thinks that keeping it under the principal's desk was such a waste when it *should* be out in front of the world for *everyone* to see."

"Out in front of the world?" I asked, stepping around Principal Davis's desk, keeping it between me and the rest of The Scavengers as they entered the room.

Another Scavenger spoke as she took a place at the front of the group. "Where it is doesn't matter. All that matters now is that we're here with you, Chase."

I didn't like how The Scavengers knew my name.

The girl reached for me with her hand. "*Join* us, Chase..." she hissed. "*Play* with us... forever..."

Uh, yeah, *super* creepy!

I backed up, feeling another gust of cold air from the open window that was about as high as my waist. The whole thing was shaped like a rectangle about four-feet wide by one foot tall, I think.

It faced the front parking lot, which meant that the front doors of the school were right outside, around the corner to the left. And underneath all the front office windows were shrubberies with prickly needles.

The Scavengers continued to slowly move forward, reaching their hands out and wiggling their fingers slowly at me. The last time I had a run in with these kids, it wasn't nearly as creepy. Victor must've given the order to take their "freak-people-out" game to the next level.

And I didn't even want to know what would happen if they actually got ahold of me, so I backed up until my body bumped against the wall.

I raised my hand and pretended to tip a hat that wasn't there. "G'day to y'all!" I said, and then rolled across the bottom edge of the window.

Friday. 7:40 AM. Outside.

As I landed behind the shrubs outside Principal Davis's office, I could hear The Scavengers rush toward the open window, but they were too late. I was already crawling across the dirt along the side of the building.

Other students were just getting to school and walking along the sidewalk, toward the front doors of the building.

All I needed to do was take my mask off and wait for a break in the crowd so I could step out without being seen.

The last thing I needed was for someone to be like, "Dude, what're you doing in the bushes?"

Knowing the way my brain worked, I probably would've tried to make a joke by saying something like, "Going number one!" No wait, that's not even bad enough. It would've been more like, "Going number *two!*"

I watched, waiting for my moment to jump from the bushes, but it didn't look like it was coming anytime soon. The crowd of students just grew thicker as the seconds ticked by.

At that moment, someone clutched my mask at the top of my head. My hands snapped up, grabbing the bottom of the mask before it was pulled off my face, and then I dropped to my back so whoever was holding onto me would let go.

133

I expected to see The Scavengers in the bushes behind me, but of course my luck couldn't be that awesome. Instead, it was a small pack of red ninjas wearing their new masks.

"You've gotta be kidding me," I grunted, shooting myself through the red ninjas and toward the exact opposite direction of where the front doors were.

The red ninjas seemed to be everywhere at all times, but in the shrubs outside the school? No, one of them *had* to have seen me fall out the window.

And if those kids were like any other kids on the planet, they'd have a cellphone on them. I figured I only had *minutes* to get into the school before they sent a mass text to the other ninjas in their clan. I had to hurry if I didn't want an entire army of red ninjas chasing after me, trying to take my mask as some sort of prize.

I sprinted against the side of the building, pretty much not caring if anyone from the parking lot saw me that time. Getting spotted was better than getting caught by the ninjas who were hot on my tail.

"Just give us your mask!" one of the red ninjas ordered. "That's all we want! Give it to us and we'll let you go!"

"Nope!" I hollered.

At the side of the school, I dug my foot into the dirt and dashed to my right, still running behind the shrubs. The footsteps following me made me push even harder.

I wasn't sure where I was headed, but does anyone when they're getting chased by ninjas? Was that even a question that normal people asked themselves?

The side doors to the school were coming up quick, but with my mask still on my face, I couldn't use that entrance. My only shot was getting to the back of the school where nobody else was going to be, over to where the dumpsters were.

I slowed a little, but not so much that the ninjas behind me could catch up. They were still several yards away, and all I had to do was make sure I didn't trip over the spot where the sidewalk started.

At the doors, I leapt like a gazelle through the air, trying to clear the concrete walkway.

At the same time, someone forced open the doors, smashing them against me. My super heroic escape came to a stop in the blink of an eye.

I fell against the cold hard concrete, hearing footsteps gather around me. I pushed myself up, staring at all the dirty sneakers of the other kids standing nearby.

A few sneakers were caked in dirt – the shoes of the red ninjas who had been following me.

But the sneakers from the other kids were clean – the ones who had opened the door.

I looked up, expecting to see more red ninjas, but instead, got an eyeful of something I'd never seen before.

Three kids hovered over me. All I could see were their eyes through their ninja masks that were pulled over their heads – their *green* ninja masks.

The three new ninjas were wearing green masks that had two parts to them – a piece of cloth over the head, and then a second piece of cloth tied around their eyes. They were wearing armor, but it was the kind of armor that motocross guys wear – the hard plastic shell that went over their chest and shoulders.

First red ninjas, and now green ninjas? Wyatt had mentioned that I shouldn't be surprised if I saw a new ninja clan sprout up, but that was easier said than done. I *was* surprised.

And honestly, I held back a laugh that was brewing somewhere in my throat. Red and green ninjas standing next to each other made it look like it was Christmas. I was being chased by Christmas ninjas!

That only lasted about a second though because all six ninjas dove for my mask at the same time.

My mind went blank, and my muscles took over. I somersaulted before any of the ninjas could touch me.

GREEN NINJAS! YOU'LL HAVE TO TRUST ME AGAIN... ...THEY'RE GREEN.

As they bumped heads and crashed into each other, I rolled to my feet, and started running across the grass, in front of the entire world to see. A couple adults stared from their cars as I dashed across the lawn. A few of them even raised their cellphones to take a pic. Being the ham that I am, I waved.

I cut around the last turn I needed to make before I could see the dumpsters far off in the distance. All I had to do was make it there so I could sneak into the cafeteria doors. The only thing standing between the dumpsters and me was the staff parking lot.

I ran hard, pumping my fists with each stride. The red and green ninjas had rejoined the chase and were now gaining on me.

Slipping down the side of a bunch of SUV's, I thought that maybe I could lose them for a second. The dumpsters were too far away so I knew I had to try something else.

Lowering myself on the pavement, I scanned under all the cars. Six ninjas had been chasing after me, so I saw twelve feet coming to a stop a few cars down.

"Where'd he go?"

"I don't know! He just disappeared!"

"He didn't just disappear, you dolt! He's here somewhere. He's just hiding."

"What if he made it to the school already?"

"Good point. Let's split up. Red ninjas will search the parking lot. Green ninjas will check around the dumpsters next to the school."

"Dangit!" I said under my breath while clenching my jaw. "Don't go to the dumpsters!"

Trying to lose the ninjas in the parking lot wasn't going to work since they were splitting up.

Pushing myself off the pavement, I started running again, trying to make it so all the ninjas saw me. That way, they'd chase after me together instead of splitting into two groups again. My only shot at the dumpsters was to make it so they were all behind me.

"Hey, Christmas ninjas!" I bellowed, jumping up and down while I ran. "Santa called! He's pretty unhappy that a bunch of his elves quit their jobs to become ninjas!"

Just as I'd hoped, all six of the ninjas started coming after me again.

At least in a parking lot full of cars, I didn't have to try and be faster than anyone. All I needed to do was wind back and forth between the parked cars and keep moving forward.

The ninjas split apart, running between cars to get to me. As long as they stayed in a cluster behind me, there was a chance I could get away in one piece.

I ran to the back of one row of cars, and dashed down the parking lot before cutting back into the line of cars.

The ninjas were still on my trail, but my plan was working. The parked cars made perfect obstacles.

And then, at that moment, the kids wearing vulture

masks appeared from behind a dark green minivan.

In my mind, I saw the world as a video game. "The Scavengers have joined your party!"

I bumbled to a stop, looking back and forth between the ninjas behind me and The Scavengers in front of me.

If I were in some sort of movie, a helicopter would appear at the very last second, pulling me to safety, but I totes wasn't in a movie.

Forcing myself to move, I ran down the side of two parked cars, trying to get a grip on where I was in the parking lot. The dumpsters were much closer than I thought; they were only about twenty cars away from where I was standing.

I quickly scanned the sidewalk to see if there was anything I could use to help me escape, but there wasn't. It was just a bare sidewalk.

The only thing I could do was run as hard as I could and hope I was faster than all the kids who were after me.

And then I saw it. From where I was crouched in the parking lot, I saw the side door of the cafeteria. It was the one that opened to the backstage.

Victor, all by himself, was wheeling my covered project through the door!

Principal Davis said someone would help take it from the garage to the stage, and if Victor had volunteered to do it, then of course the principal would be cool with it. Davis didn't know Victor was insane.

Victor caught me from the corner of his eye. When he noticed me, he LOL'd.

I didn't waste another second. The ninjas and The Scavengers were so close I could see their puffs of breath in the air behind the cars nearby.

Shooting back to my feet, I sprinted harder than I ever had in my entire life. My feet were going to kill me in the morning, but all I'd have to do was tell them I was sorry by soaking them in hot water. My feet were always suckers for hot water.

My sneakers hit the ground at a hundred miles an hour as I shot across the sidewalk.

The Scavengers were easy to lose first since they were all wearing those weirdo vulture masks. Most of them had to stop because they could barely see anything through the tiny eyeholes. Noobs.

It was the ninjas I had to worry about, and in a wide-open space, those kids were *fast*.

My feet stomped across the pavement as I got closer to the cafeteria.

I made it past five cars with only fifteen more to go. If each car was five feet wide, then that was, like, seventy-five feet I still had to run, which to me was a million miles!

I ran fast, but the ninjas ran faster.

Ten cars to go.

They say you're never supposed to look behind you when you're racing because it'll slow you down. Whoever said that was right.

Glancing over my shoulder, I saw all six ninjas, like, right behind me.

That was it. I was toast. I still had about fifty feet to go.

It was impossible.

...

Until I realized I could get rid of all the ninjas more easily than I thought. The ninjas didn't want *me*. They wanted my *mask*.

I felt so stupid. I could just get another mask from my locker! I had tons of them!

Ripping my ninja mask off my face, I tossed it into the air like that lady at weddings who throws flowers to a bunch of other ladies.

The next few seconds were a blur because I wasn't about to look back to see if the other ninjas took the bait.

I slowed to a stop at the dumpsters since they were just outside the cafeteria, and I didn't want anyone see me running through the windows.

Catching my breath, I looked behind me.

There was nothing. The red and the green ninjas had disappeared, along with my ninja mask. The Scavengers were gone too, but I knew those guys couldn't have been far. If there was one thing I've learned since meeting The Scavengers, it was that they were never far... ever.

Friday. 8:00 AM. The cafeteria.

I waited until I wasn't breathing like a fat cat before entering the cafeteria. I didn't want to attract any attention, but after seeing the whirlwind of students in the room, I wasn't sure I could if I tried.

The cafeteria was so packed with kids that it was almost impossible to move around. It was as if the entire school had been crammed into that room.

And then I remembered that it wasn't just the sixth graders there for the assembly. It was also the seventh and eighth graders. That's why it felt like I was in a mosh pit at a rock concert.

The stage curtain at the front of the lunchroom was completely shut. Zoe, Faith, and Principal Davis were at the short staircase on the right side of the stage, nodding and saying a bunch of stuff to each other. All three of them looked excited for the assembly to start.

The clock on the back wall said it was eight-o-clock sharp, which meant that the curtains would probably open at any time.

Gidget, Slug, and Brayden were standing against the wall right under the clock.

141

I jumped as high as I could a few times to see over the heads of the taller seventh and eighth graders. What was wrong with those kids? There were seats everywhere! Take a seat already!

Victor was nowhere in sight, but I didn't care. All I cared about was getting to my project that had to have been on the stage. Victor wheeled it in, and I'm pretty sure it wasn't because he wanted to help out.

The three pieces of broken statue had been taken from Principal Davis's office, and after seeing Victor with my project, it didn't take too long for my brain to catch up... the broken head of James Buchanan was going to be somewhere on my project for the whole world to see when Principal Davis opened those curtains.

"Morning, Chase," a voice said as I tried weaseling my way through the crowd.

I turned around. It was Victor.

"You should find a good seat," Victor said. "The show's about to begin."

Victor held a bag of popcorn with one hand while stuffing his other hand inside it. I'm not sure if he was eating the snack or just running his fingers through it. Either way, it was weird.

"What did you do?" I said, pushing my way through the crowd, toward him.

"You'll find out soon enough," Victor said as he smiled. There were bits of half chewed popcorn in his teeth.

"You said you weren't going to do anything like this!" I said. "You told me your plan *wasn't* to make anyone hate me!"

The other kids around Victor and me starting looking at us because of how loud I was.

Victor smiled while pressing his lips together. His eyes closed halfway as his eyebrows raised on his forehead. He sort of looked like a duck. "I lied," he said coldly.

Zoe's voice came from the speaker system. "Alriiiiiiiight, everybody!" she said into her microphone. "It looks like it's about time for us to start, so if all of you could find a seat, we'll get things going!"

At once, everyone in the cafeteria started moving toward all the chairs that were set up for the show.

I turned back to Victor so I could try and talk some sense into him, but he was gone.

Now that all the students behind me had found a chair, I could see over all their heads. Naomi was standing in the back of the room, pointing her cellphone in front of her, filming the assembly. When she saw me, she lowered her phone.

My ex-best friend and I stared at each other for what seemed like forever.

Finally, I mouthed the words, "Help me!"

That's when Naomi looked away.

Most of the students in front of me, closer to the stage, had taken their seats. It was only me and a handful of other kids who were still standing in the crowd.

Zoe was up front with Faith by her side. I knew that Zoe didn't have a clue about everything that happened during the week, but I wasn't sure about Faith. Was it possible that she was doing her own thing behind the scenes? Like, I had been working behind the scenes, but was Faith working *behind* behind the scenes? Did I even just say that right?

From the smile shining on Faith's face, I was pretty sure she was clueless though. She had been so busy helping Zoe with the Bash that I barely got to talk to her at all that week.

A long line of light peeked out at the bottom of the curtain, where the velvet fabric hung half an inch above the old wooden boards of the stage. The light stopped right at the center, and then started a few feet over again. The shadow that broke the line of light was my project. It had to have been.

I started pushing through the kids in their seats, trying my best to not look frantic. All I had to do was get to Zoe, explain the "*sitch*," and then fix whatever Victor did to my project while the curtain was still closed. After that, everything could go on perfectly normal. It was a pretty simple solution actually.

Except I was halfway across the room when Zoe spoke into the mic again. "Students of Buchanan Schooooooool," she said, almost singing. "I'd like to welcome all of you to our assembly! As you know, our Bash is going to be held directly after school today, but we're here right now to get you *pumped!* We've got a little taste of what to expect tonight with some talent acts, games, and a couple prizes, but first..."

Uh oh...

Zoe grabbed at the thick, braided rope in front of the velvet curtain at the side of the stage, and starting pulling down on it.

143

Everything inside me went into the panic mode as I started racing through the students to get to my cousin before she opened the curtain.

Zoe laughed, huffing and puffing as she stopped pulling the rope. She pretended to wipe the sweat off her brow. Most of the room laughed at the joke.

Faith took the part of the rope behind Zoe and together, they both pulled back, obviously putting all their weight into it because they both leaned over so far that the only thing holding them up was the rope itself.

The velvet curtain at the center of the stage shook slightly, and then start splitting open slowly.

I turned toward the middle of the stage and started running faster. It was too late to stop Zoe and Faith from pulling on the rope, so the only other thing I could think of was to try and hold both sides of the curtain shut.

I flew to the front of the stage as the curtain split open a little more. My project was right behind the fabric, and I could see just what Victor had done.

The broken pieces of the statue were sitting on the sign at the very top of the entryway I had built.

At the very last second, I jumped onto the wooden stage,

and grabbed both sides of the red velvet curtain, pulling them shut so I could keep my project hidden.

I used every ounce of muscle in my lanky arms to get the curtain to shut again, but the whole thing must've been built to open easily after a certain point. Even though Zoe and Faith struggled to get the first part moving, after about six inches, some gears helped with the rest.

Zoe and Faith let go of the rope from the side of the stage, gasping when they saw me. I probably looked like I was trying to be a class clown or something.

I clenched my fists around the red velvet fabric, but the curtain was already opening on its own.

I refused to let go, but my arms opened so wide that it felt like my bones were about to break, and then I was thrown to the side of the wooden stage, sliding to a stop in front of the entire school.

The room of students gasped when they saw the head of James Buchanan at the top of my project. Even Zoe and Faith screamed, but it might've been because they were afraid they had hurt me.

I didn't move. I just let the sounds of all the angry voices fill my world as I stared at the project I had worked so hard on.

Victor had won. The Scavengers had won.

Through my blurry vision, I saw two kids climb on the stage toward me. When they were close enough, I saw that it was two hall monitors in suits.

Principal Davis took the broken pieces of statue off my project and cradled them in his hands. He looked at me, disappointed and shaking his head.

I slid myself off the stage, onto the cafeteria floor, at the very front of all the students yelling at me. Everyone had been pretty upset about the broken statue all week, but I had no idea just how upset.

"How could you do something like that to our statue?"

"Don't you have any sense of respect for President Buchanan's memory?"

"Take him away! Get him outta here!"

I started defending myself, but it was useless. The mob was so loud that nobody could even hear me.

Zoe and Faith stared at me from the side of the stage. Both of their jaws were dropped as the two hall monitors started to walk me down the front of the cafeteria.

I only hoped that my cousin would at least hear my part of the story before joining the club of kids who hated me, which at that point, was the entire school. I'd kept everything about The Scavengers a secret from her since I learned about them, but I was beginning to think that was a mistake.

How was it going to sound when I started blaming a mysterious group of students that almost nobody knew about? Crazy – that's how. It would be like blaming a bunch of ghosts!

I looked around at the faces of everyone shouting at me. Gidget, Slug, and Brayden were still at the back. I couldn't believe Brayden was even back there – this whole thing was partly because of him!

Naomi wasn't standing in the spot that I had last seen her.

Victor was near the other end of the stage, shouting at me, along with the other kids around him.

He did it. He finished what The Scavengers started a few weeks back. I was defeated – *pwned*, and blinking in and out of existence. If I was lucky, maybe I'd respawn at my old school… no, too bad that's not how real life worked.

I wasn't sure if there was any way I could come back from total, utter humiliation. I'd probably have to switch schools, or grow a mustache so nobody would recognize me ever again.

…and then the microphone screamed with feedback as

someone stomped across the stage.

The two hall monitors, who were walking me out, stopped in place. Even Principal Davis spun around at the terrible screech over the speaker system.

"*Chase didn't do this!*" a girl's voice spoke into the mic. It was Naomi… staring right at me.

"He was set up by an eighth grader named Victor!" she continued quickly. "Everything you know of Chase Cooper is a lie! He's *not* the villain! He's *not* the bad guy that everyone thinks he is, and he doesn't deserve *any* of this hate!"

I stared at Naomi.

And then she dropped the bomb. "Victor is the leader of The Scavengers! Yes, they're real, and they're a bunch of wads!"

Victor boomed some nonsense from the crowd, and then dove across the wood of the stage.

Naomi stepped backward, but she was safe. The hall monitors who had been next to me grabbed Victor before he got too far.

Victor's earing dropped to the floor and bounced a

couple times. Some kids gagged when they saw it, but started laughing when they realized the earing was a fake clip-on.

My ex-best friend looked at Principal Davis as she held out her cellphone. "I've got all the proof on video here. I've been filming everything for the past week... Chase is innocent."

The roomful of students quieted down. The only sound came from Victor screaming about how Naomi was lying, but I'm pretty sure everyone could tell *he* was the one who was lying from the way he was acting.

Naomi walked to the side of the stage and handed the microphone back to my cousin.

I was surprised that Victor wasn't freaking out by running away. I guess some kids just knew when they had lost the game. He wasn't a *total* sore loser.

Principal Davis put his hand on my shoulder and asked me to wait in the lobby so he could get Naomi and try to figure everything out with just the three of us. He set the pieces of broken statue on a bench right outside the cafeteria doors.

Victor finally calmed down as the hall monitors took him out of the cafeteria. He shot me the worst look I've ever gotten from anyone in my life. It was even *worse* than Jesse's evil eye.

"This isn't over," he said. "This is just the beginning..."

"Nope," Principal Davis said from the door as Naomi stood by his side. "It's over."

Victor said nothing.

"Take him into the front office and have someone call his parents," the principal said to the hall monitors. "We're gonna get to the bottom of this if it takes all day."

The two hall monitors nodded, and took Victor away.

Victor didn't argue.

Principal Davis turned to Naomi and me. "I need the two of you to wait out here for a minute. I need to let Zoe know that she can continue with the assembly so the students don't sit and fester."

A second later, the principal was gone, and it was just Naomi and me in the lobby.

There was a moment of silence before Naomi finally broke the ice, but not by speaking. She unzipped her book bag and took out the teacup that had been glued back together.

Handing me the teacup, she said, "I want you to have

this."

"But…" I started to say.

"No," she said, interrupting me. "I need you take it. I need you to forgive me. I need for us to be friends again. I need you to know I'm sorry… for everything."

I stared at Naomi. She wore a smile, but also looked like she was going to cry.

The teacup made a "*CLINK*" sound. Naomi had put a stick of gold sparkly glue inside the cup. She was giving me both.

"I needed to make things right," Naomi said. "A few weeks ago, during the election, I watched you stand in front of the school, ready to sacrifice yourself to stop The Scavengers… and when I saw you on that stage today, I knew that it was my turn. It was the only way to make it up to you."

I looked at the teacup in my hand. "I'm not sure what to say…" I whispered honestly.

Naomi smiled. "You don't need to say anything."

Gidget, Slug, and Brayden appeared in the doorway of the cafeteria. Zoe and Faith were on the stage, making jokes and performing some skits for the rest of the students in the school.

Gidget was texting on her phone. Slug looked half asleep again, but Brayden… was *smiling* at me.

"Why are you smiling like that?" I said to him. "*You're* the one behind all this! I saw those photos of you giving

Naomi the statue!"

Brayden's smile disappeared. "Oh, dude," he said, shocked. "I only did that because you said you wished The Scavengers would make a move! Remember? You said that at the beginning of the week!"

"I…" I said, and then stopped. *"What?"*

Gidget pointed at Brayden. "He's right. I remember that. You totes said that to us."

My mind flashed through my brain bank, trying to find the folder that had the conversation from Monday. "Oh, man," I said, remembering. "Dude, that was a *joke!"*

"Could've fooled us," Gidget said. "I thought you were serious too."

I slapped my forehead as everyone laughed around me.

"So you guys are really done with the ninja clan?" I asked.

Slug stepped forward, wiping the sleep from his eyes. I wasn't sure how he could flip back and forth between fast asleep and wide-awake, but it was a secret I was determined to learn. "Done with the ninja clan?" he asked. "Are you kidding me? After that *insane* scene in the cafeteria? There's no way this thing is as boring as I thought! Forget the football team! I'm a ninja for life!"

"Good," I said. "Because I have a feeling things are going to get worse soon."

My ninja clan looked at me, puzzled.

"I'll just say," I said, repeating the words of Wyatt. "Don't be surprised if you see another ninja clan pop up soon. I'm pretty sure we're about to have some pretty big ninja problems."

Gidget smiled. "Nice."

The principal stepped out of the cafeteria and let the doors shut behind him. He asked Gidget, Slug, and Brayden to go back into the assembly since there wasn't any reason for them to be in the lobby.

Principal Davis glanced at the door to the front office, and then spoke. "Naomi, why don't you come in first, and explain exactly what in the world has been going on. I'll need to see all the footage on your phone that you talked about on the stage."

Naomi smiled. "Sure. I'll tell you everything, Mr. Davis."

"Chase, wait out here for a minute," he said. "I'll call you in after I speak with Naomi."

I nodded.

Principal Davis and Naomi stepped through the doors to the front office, and just like that, the lobby was empty. It was just the broken statue of President Buchanan and me.

I crashed on one of the benches out there, leaning against the wall, and let out a humongous sigh of relief. The weight of The Scavengers was off my shoulders, and I felt so light that I was afraid I'd float away.

Brayden wasn't the bad guy I thought he was, and Naomi had switched sides again.

I knew that I should've had hard feelings about Naomi, but I didn't. Those feelings were gone and I was happy to get rid of them.

Spinning the cup in my hand, I studied the spots where Naomi had used gold colored glue to piece it back together. Kintsugi is what Naomi had called it. The teacup was more beautiful because of its history – it was now unique among a billion other cups just like it.

The friendship Naomi and I had was broken, cracked apart just like that cup, but Naomi was trying to glue it back together. I just needed to let her.

She used to be one of my best friends before everything that happened, but I suspected our friendship was going to be even stronger now because it's been glued back together.

That goes for my ninja clan too. We've been through a lot with a lot more to come, but it was stronger because of our struggle to survive as a team, and my own struggle to be a leader. I might've lost my mask earlier that morning, but there was no way I was finished with being a sixth grade ninja.

Nope, if I could be a sixth grade ninja for the rest of my life, I totes would.

I felt unstoppable for once.

Whatever was going on with Wyatt and the red and green ninjas would show its ugly face soon enough. But I knew that with my best buds behind me, I could stand up to anything – especially now that Naomi and I were friends again.

The glue stick inside Naomi's teacup clinked on the side. I took it out and opened it, studying the little sparkles.

The broken pieces of James Buchanan's head sat on the bench next to me, and I was struck with an idea…

Let's just say I "fixed" the statue.

Kintsugi!

Stories – what an incredible way to open one's mind to a fantastic world of adventure. It's my hope that this story has inspired you in some way, lighting a fire that maybe you didn't know you had. Keep that flame burning no matter what. It represents your sense of adventure and creativity, and that's something nobody can take from you. Thanks for reading! If you enjoyed this book, I ask that you help spread the word by sharing it or leaving an honest review!

- Marcus
m@MarcusEmerson.com

AND DON'T FORGET TO CHECK OUT
TOTES SWEET HERO!

TOTES SWEET HERO ALSO INCLUDES THE BONUS SHORT COMIC
diary of a 6th grade ninja STINK BUG SABOTAGE

Marcus Emerson is the author of several highly imaginative children's books including the 6th Grade Ninja series, Secret Agent 6th Grader, and Totes Sweet Hero. His goal is to create children's books that are engaging, funny, and inspirational for kids of all ages - even the adults who secretly never grew up.

Marcus Emerson is currently having the time of his life with his beautiful wife and their four amazing children. He still dreams of becoming an astronaut someday and walking on Mars.

Made in the USA
Middletown, DE
09 December 2021

54820095R00097